Rosemary Achaius

Friend & Protector
of the
Last Neugle
[The Early Years]

Catherine J Meldrum

Cover Illustrator
Annie Parr

Acknowledgements

For All My Family

To My Husband
Thank you, Mimis,
for your Patience and Encouragement,

To My Daughter
Thank You Caroline, for Reading, Re-reading, and
Reading again: Thank you for your constant
encouragement, pushing me forward with your
enthusiasm, every time I was about to give up.

A Special Thanks To
Annie Parr
For Being Inside My Head
When Creating the Cover Illustration
Thank You
Kitty Donovan
For your Encouraging Review
of the First Draft under the Original Name of
King Frost & The Merrykiss
Thank You
Alexandra Skinner
Fiona MacLeay
Georgie Brown
Heather Craig
Jeanette Graham
Lynne McDonald
Orla Johnston
Shirley Logan
For Your Reviews & Constructive Comments

Rosemary Achaius Friend & Protector of the Last Neugle.

Foreword

Dear Readers
Rosy begins telling Hanna and James a story which
took place in the past. To save any confusion, I have
written their present timeline conversations, etc., in
bold text.
I hope you will enjoy Rosemary's early Years and
will look forward to the continuation of Rosy's story
'Things Don't Just Disappear.'

Kind Regards
Catherine

A Noisy Dilemma

Rosy was just about at breaking point listening to the children constantly bickering. They argued about everything, no matter the subject. It reminded her of a story her mother told her when she was a child. A story about another brother and sister who used to argue about everything. She called out to them and patted the soft cushions, on either side of her, on the large sofa.

"James, Hanna, come and sit here and I'll tell you a story."

Maybe if she told them a story, perhaps, just perhaps, there would be some peace in the house for an hour or two. She tried to think of a story that would hold their attention; maybe one of her mother's stories would do the trick. Her mother's stories always came with a meaning which tended to make you stop and think. Then it came to her, and why not tell them that story, she thought, as if trying to convince herself.

"Are you settled...comfy... okay...I'm going to tell you the story of Rosemary Achaius."

"That's a strange name," said Hanna.

"Achaius means, 'Friend of a horse', Hanna, which in a way I suppose is a bit strange, because horses are what Rosemary loved most of all."

"I love horses too!"

"I love them more than you do!" sniped James.

"Well, then, we can all agree on something can't we, we all love horses!"

"Now then, there are many different parts to Rosemary's story so it's a bit difficult to know where to begin, because if I start at the beginning it will make it a very long story. If I don't, you might not understand everything. So, what do you think?"

"I don't care how long it takes," James said, "I want to hear it all, right from the beginning."

Hanna said nothing, she just gave a little nod of her head, not wishing to show her agreement with her brother.

"Okay then, but before I begin, I should really give you an introduction as to who's who and tell you a little bit about where this story takes place."

"So where to begin…In Scotland, I suppose."

"No!" Said James.

"A story should always begin, 'Once Upon A Time'."

They all laughed, and the story began…

Once upon a time, tucked away in the Grampian Mountains, in the highlands of Scotland, there was a magical place called the Kingdom of Frost.
It wasn't a very big Kingdom, but it was a very special one to all who lived there.

James smiled.

In the middle of the Kingdom, was a small village called, Lakeside.

Lakeside was in the County of Merry and cradled one of the many tiny lochs hidden in the Grampian valleys. To any stranger stumbling across it for the first time, it looked the same as any other small village.   In fact, Rosemary's description when anyone asked, was always short and to the point.

'Nothing much to see, just an old castle, a loch and a hundred houses.'

But that description couldn't have been further from the truth because Lakeside, like the rest of the

Kingdom of Frost, was a place of wonder; a place of excitement; and a truly magical place to live.

Lakeside wasn't what you would call a sleepy village, but then nor did it run at a fast pace: although it did in the summer.   In the summer, it had so many visitors that sometimes, it looked like a town.

People in cars, vans, and on motorbikes arrived daily. Families came with caravans; some people even brought boats on trailers.

Sometimes groups of Brownies and Scouts came from the city to camp, they'd pitch their tents in the fields surrounding the loch.

"I love camping," said Hanna.

"No you don't," argued James, "you've never been camping."

Rosy ignored them and continued...

During the busiest months of the summer, there was a weekly farmers market where you could buy everything from freshly picked fruit, to hens, and fish.

Sometimes, the local children would organise a jumble sale to raise money for a local charity; buy more fireworks for Guy Fawkes night; or for the Merry-Kiss.

Once a year, there would be a fair with a merry-go-round on the village green: that was a favourite with all the children.

The large fir tree on the green was a bit off centre, as most visitors to the village pointed out, but regardless of its position it was lovingly decorated and admired every Christmas, when the whole village watched the lighting ceremony and sung carols.

"I love Christmas, it's my favourite," said Hanna dreamily.

Rosy smiled, "Mine too Hanna"...

In the centre of the green, near the fir tree was a beautiful white bandstand. It was the pride and joy of every villager. You could sit on one of the benches at the side of the green and listen to the band rehearsing every Saturday morning.

The bandstand hadn't always been there, it had been built at the end of the war. It was the heart and soul of Lakeside, and on most days a hive of bustling activity.

Bordering the village green was a wide pavement. The pavement began at the Village Hall and ended at the Dragon's Lair Hotel with an assortment of shops in between.
The shops sold everything you could possibly need no matter the date on the calendar. It was the place

to go, if you wanted to buy groceries; meat; fish; get a haircut; post a letter; bank money; have tea; ice cream; cake; or just catch up on the village gossip.

There were two large medieval churches, one at either end of Main Street. The churches each had an adjoining portcullis which when dropped closed off the whole village and castle to intruders.

"Have you ever seen the portcullis down, Rosy?"

"No, I never have, James, but I've often wondered."

Those in charge of the churches took their turn at ringing the bells; apart from Christmas, Easter, and emergencies, when every bell in the Kingdom of Frost rang at the same time.

As you left the village on the way to the castle, there was a fork in the road. The left turn took you to the Lakeside cottages and the old water mill. If you continued, the road brought you to South Main Street Church.

If you turned right, it took you up a steep winding road to the castle.
The watermill was in desperate need of repair. Its water wheel started and stopped at odd times as if it were reminding people that it was still there.

"Why was it called, Lakeside and not Lochside," asked James?

"Good question James: I haven't a clue, but it's one to remember so we can find out later."

"Now, as you know, the family who lived in Merry Castle were really famous."

Hanna smiled at Rosy.

They were so famous they were known throughout the whole world, and in my opinion, they were one of the friendliest and most interesting families you would ever wish to meet.

The castle was given the name Merry by its owner, King Jack Frost.

The children gave her a questioning look...

"No... not that King Jack Frost," she said, and continued...

It was named Merry, because it was always full of laughter, especially in the wintertime when the King and Queen had lots of parties.

One of those special parties was, the Merry-Kiss Ball.

The Merry-Kiss was named such in celebration of the first kiss of frost throughout the Kingdom, and it was always a truly amazing night. It was the one night in the year when every person, animal, and creature, got together by a special invitation from the King. It was also one of the four nights of the year, when magic was everywhere, and everything was possible.

One of the trustees described it as, 'a jolly affair,' and believe me, it certainly was, and every year it got jollier… **she smiled**.

The Clan Frost had lived at Merry castle for many generations, but no one knew exactly how many generations because no one knew how long the castle had been there. They knew that it had been there in the days when we could see fairies, and when we were still friendly with dragons.

"Fairies… Oh how lovely!"

"Woah… Dragons… really?"

"Yes James… really! We know that, because those are some of the things that are written about in the old journals that are kept in the castle library."

"What are journals?" inquired Hanna.

"Well… I suppose they're a bit like diaries. They were written by the King's trustees, or one of their family."

The trustees were the King's most loyal friends.

Some of the trustees worked at the castle; some looked after the stables and some of them tended to the gardens and the loch. Some of them lived in the village of Lakeside, but the ones closest to the King always lived in one of seven lakeside cottages. They didn't write very much about their normal daily routine, they wrote more about other things…and well... some of their stories painted an incredible picture of Merry Castle's colourful past, that's for sure.

It's such a shame that none of the journals were ever dated. They just wrote the family name, year one, year two, etc., and the number of the cottage where they lived.

"Why is that?" Hanna asked.

"No one really knows, Hanna," Rosy replied.

"It's just always been that way. I'm sure there must be a reason, but so far, I haven't been able to find one."

"I remember when I was young reading a number two journal while I was sitting in the castle library. It was so interesting, and I tried to find the ones that followed but among the many thousands of journals written by the trustees it was too difficult. Although, I suppose not impossible if someone wanted to find a dragon story…"

She smiled and winked at James.

When a trustee retires, they must give their cottage to one of their trusted family members, but it's King Frost who has the final decision on who his new trustee will be. Then the new journals begin again, Year 1, year 2 and so on.

"Have you ever wondered how old your cottage is Rosy?"

"I did try to find out when the cottages had been built thinking that perhaps they had been built at the same time as the castle, but I had no luck so I'm not really sure if the cottages were built at the same time as the castle or not. If there's one thing that I am sure of it's this, the castle; the cottages; the water mill and the loch, have all stood witness to everything; everything that had ever happened in the Kingdom of Frost"

"Oh, if only they could speak! I'll bet these walls could tell us lots of interesting stories," said James.

"Yes, I'm sure they probably could, and a lot more exciting than this one, but we have to begin somewhere... right? So... where was I?"

"The trustees," Hanna got it in before James.

"Oh Yes!"

So, this story is about the daughter of a special trustee and how she became, among other things, the friend and protector of the very last Neugle.

"Wait... What...? A Neugle... What's a Neugle?" asked James.

"In many of the books on mythology, it's written that Neugles are from the Orkney Islands, but no-one really knows for sure because there are so many myths and legends surrounding them."

"But what is it?" Hanna asked.

"I suppose you could call it a type of water horse although it doesn't always live in the water. In fact, it's not really a horse at all, it just likes being a horse. It's actually a shapeshifter."

"A what?"

"It means it can change its shape silly," snapped James. "Oh, I wish I could shape-shift."

"Be careful what you wish for James," said Rosy, smiling... "you never know if there are faeries listening..."

"Fairies are lovely," said Hanna.

"Ah, but there are 'fairies', and then there are other 'faeries', Hanna. James is right when he

says a shapeshifter means that it can take the shape of anything that it chooses to be."

"Anything at all?"

"Yes, anything at all, even you Hanna!"

Neugles are, by nature, very mischievous; and from some of the stories written about them, we know that they really loved to play tricks on people. They didn't play nasty tricks, like some of the other water creatures, the tangies for instance, the tangies were so nasty: They didn't like humans at all. No, no, neugles just liked to have fun, they're, pure of heart. They would never hurt anyone, not deliberately anyway. So, if you ever hear a story about a bad neugle, don't believe it because it won't be true.

One of the differences between a neugle and a horse, is its tail.

No one knows why but for some reason when it turns into a horse it has a very long tail: much longer than a real horse.

"Although, come to think of it, there have been horses in history that have had tails of more than 14 feet."

"WoW... 14feet, that really is long isn't it!" exclaimed James.

"It certainly is. One of the horses was named, Linus, the Oregon Wonder Horse, and it lived in America in the early 1900s. I read about it in an old American magazine many years ago. However, the tail of a neugle is more like six or seven feet."

If a neugle wants you to think that it's a normal horse, it will coil its tail up between its back legs out of sight, and you won't know the difference. It has a beautiful extra-long double mane, which covers its large round eyes, like a chunky fringe. Its thick Mane hides its eyes, which change colour when it's happy, sad, or angry.

"Beautiful," said Hanna.

"They really are Hanna, they're one of the most beautiful creatures you will ever see," answered Rosy.

"Although, if you ever did see one, it wouldn't be until after sundown because they don't like to come out during the day. Now for the most important part, no human can ride a Neugle."

In the olden days, people who went searching for Neugles were given a stern warning never to try to mount one because its skin is covered in some sort of sticky substance and once you've mounted, you're stuck fast and cannot get back off. The neugle would think you were playing a game and because they love water would dive right into the nearest pool, and you would never be seen again.

Hanna shivered...

"I know, that's a scary thought, isn't it?"

"Anyway...back to Rosemary's story...

Red Hair and Rosy Cheeks

Rosemary's parents, Victoria, and Henry Achaius, moved to Lakeside village in 1935, the same year that the Royal twins were born. Their cottage had been a wedding gift from Henry's grandfather, which meant that Henry was to be the next trustee. Henry and his wife Victoria loved the cottage but really had no intention of making it their forever home. Henry loved the hustle and bustle of the city too much. However, we all know that sometimes plans can change. In this case it was the start of World War two.

War was declared in 1939 and all the young men from Lakeside village left for six months of army training before being sent to their army, navy, or air force unit. Henry was among the married men and therefore not called up immediately.

*

Their daughter Rosemary came into the world just after midnight on Friday the 13 of December 1940. Victoria had been enjoying the Merry-Kiss and had not had enough time to make the journey to the

23

maternity hospital in the city, so Rosemary was born in number 1 Lakeside Cottages. The King said that Rosemary was one of the privileged, because there had only been two others born in number one.

Victoria and Henry were thrilled and named their new baby girl after both of their grandmothers, Rose, and Mary. Although, after a few days Henry shortened her name to Rosy, because he said it matched her little rosy cheeks and bright red hair.

"Woah wait a minute… your name's Rosy and your hair is red: is this story about you?" James questioned her, smiling.

"I'll tell you what, James, you listen carefully and tell me if it sounds like it's me, or not, and I'll tell you at the end if you're right!"

"Yes... but... wait: if you are Rosy, then you've met a neugle?"

"Shall I stop or continue?" Teased Rosy.

"Continue, please," said James punching his cushion.

They lived happily at the cottage for more than a year, oblivious to the fact that there was a war on, until one morning the army postman arrived with Henry's orders. He was to report for training, immediately. It was the news that Victoria had been dreading: Henry had to leave the next day.

No news was heard from him from the day he left.
It was just over a year later when Victoria received a
war office telegram. Everyone in the village had
come to dread receiving a telegram, and Victoria
knew before she opened it that the news would not
be good. She could only see the words 'Henry' and
'missing.' As you can imagine, she was distraught.

**"Oh, poor Rosy doesn't have a father now, that's
so sad," Hanna was close to tears.**

"Don't worry Hanna the story gets happier. ..."

...Victoria put on a brave face in front of Rosy, who
was too young to understand, but in her alone times
she allowed herself to grieve for him. She gave
some thought to going back to her mother's house in
the city so that she wouldn't feel so alone, but
because of the war, the cottage at Lakeside, seemed
a much safer place for Rosy and her to be. Besides,
she really believed that one day, Henry would be
found and come home. When that day came, she
wanted them to be there.

By the time the war ended in 1945, she and Rosy
loved the cottage so much that she couldn't bring
herself to leave it, she just could not imagine them
living anywhere else.

*

The cottage, being number one, was the first house you came to at the bottom of the steep winding road from the castle. It was the closest to the loch, and directly opposite the old watermill.

The back of their cottage had the most beautiful rose garden, with every type and colour of rose you could imagine and adding to the scent of the roses, was a border of every kind of herb. 'Herbs are needed for good health and tasty cooking,' was Rosy's mother's motto and she used the herbs daily.

The front of the cottage had a delightful rich green lawn with a white wooden bench at one corner, made for Victoria by Rosemary's father. It matched nicely with the white picket fence that began and ended at the rose covered archway over the gate.

When Victoria sat on the bench it always gave her a feeling of peace. She would watch Rosy play and breathe in the spectacular view of the whole loch. Victoria referred to the bench as the love seat because of her special memories. She had been sitting on the bench the day that Henry had proposed marriage to her, and on the day that King Frost had made him a trustee.

*

As the years rolled by, Rosy spent many hours sitting on the love seat chatting to the birds or counting the many different types of butterflies that visited the garden.

Every evening the King would ride by, on one of his many horses, and wave to her.

Several times a week he would stop and chat to her mother, and sometimes... quite often in fact, his white horse would arrive outside the gate without him. It would whinny and neigh at her, from the gate, until she went inside to get an apple or a carrot.

Rosy really looked forward to seeing it, and in the late afternoon she would stand on the wooden stile by the gate to wait for its arrival.

Its mane was always hanging like a thick fringe covering its eyes and Rosy would pin it to the side with her mother's hair clip like she did with her dolls. One time she gathered the hair on either side of its eyes with elastic bands, like two little bunches. Sometimes when it arrived, its eyes were blue and sometimes they were green, but many times they flashed with all the colours of the rainbow: especially if Rosy had apples.

On the day before her sixth birthday, she was standing in the garden watching her mother down at the loch side, when a boy and girl arrived at the gate. Rosy thought that they were in fancy dress costumes for the Merry-Kiss Ball, but later found out that they were Prince John and Princess Jaclyn, the children of King Frost. She remembered hearing her mother on the telephone saying that they had done something naughty and needed help.

"Oh, what did they do, to make Mrs Achaius call them naughty?" asked James.

"To tell you the whole story, we have to go back to a year earlier, to the end of the war, when the villagers were waiting for the soldiers to return."

Troublesome Traditions

It had all started in December 1945, at the end of the war, just before Rosy's fifth birthday…A telegram had arrived the first week in December to say that the soldiers would be returning home on the 10 of December. The village had been buzzing with the news, and everyone was so excited. Excited because the war was over, and their husbands and sons would soon be returning home.

Rosy's mum knew that her husband wouldn't be among the returning soldiers, which made it a sad day for her, but she was genuinely pleased for the other wives and mothers, and so happy that the war was over.

The village Christmas tree was not due to be decorated until the 13 of December.

"Why did they have to wait so long to decorate the tree?" asked Hanna.

"Because of the Merry-Kiss, silly!" James replied.

"Actually James, it wasn't. There's an old saying, they call it an old wives' tale, they say that a Christmas tree should never be decorated before the twelfth day before Christmas Day, and it must always be taken down before the twelfth day after, or there will be a whole year of bad luck."

"Oh, I don't believe in that: do you believe in that Rosy?" asked James.

Rosy didn't answer, she just gave him a knowing look before continuing...

...Someone suggested that decorating the tree early would make a wonderful festive homecoming for the returning soldiers. Perhaps they could even choose one of the soldiers to put the star on the tree. Someone else suggested a carol service.

After a long discussion by the members of the village council, it was agreed that the decorating was to be done on the 9th, four days early.

That was a decision that every council member would come to regret.

The fir tree in the centre of village green was beautifully decorated and excitement filled every house as families awaited the return of their sons, fathers, and husbands. This was to be one of the best Christmases ever. The Merry-Kiss had been early, and everyone was hoping for a white Christmas.

At first no one made the connection, when the little things went wrong, after all it was just an old wives' tale, right!

No one really believed that bad luck would happen if the decorating for Christmas was done before the twelfth day. However, on the day the soldiers were due to arrive home, the biggest blizzard in recorded history hit the County. Trains and buses were cancelled and there were no food deliveries. The village was completely cut off from the outside world for weeks and by the time the roads were passable, the shops were all closed, due to bare shelves. Those in the village who had extra shared, but everyone agreed that it was the worst Christmas ever. Even the eldest of the villagers said that they had never known anything like it. It was as if Christmas had been cancelled. It definitely didn't measure up to the wonderful Christmas that they had all been expecting that's for sure.

The New Year celebrations were the quietest the village had ever known, but everyone knew that was because there had been no beer and spirit deliveries to the local public house.

*

During the weeks of January, February, March, strange things continued happening, in fact all through the rest of the year.

First there was a fire in the village hall, then the tree on the green was struck by lightning, hence the reason the new tree being planted off centre.

Then Farmer Anderson's sheep were worried by a stray dog, and he lost half his lambs.

The loch flooded onto Rosy's front garden for the first time ever in its history, and people were crazy with worry, wondering what was going to happen next.

They did their best to stay cheerful and positive, but it was a very difficult time for many. Their one and only joy was listening to the village band rehearsing in the new bandstand on the village green, because there had been no music in the village during all the years while the men were away. The Bandstand had been a labour of love, built from the wood left over from the rebuilding of the new village hall, and it had been dedicated to those who didn't return from the war. It was the 'something good' the village had needed, and it cheered everyone up after the terrible Christmas they'd had. It was voted unanimously by all that the Christmas carols would be sung there every year. It was even suggested that they might hold a summer concert. The smiles and happiness had lasted a week or two, until gale force winds ruined a whole crop of apples.

Then, the village library lost a quarter of their books when a water pipe burst.

Every month there was one disaster after another until, at last, it was December again. Everyone was awaiting The Merry-Kiss. The Merry-Kiss, with all its beautiful patterns of frost on the windowpanes, the trees wearing their sparkling frosty dresses: all of nature awaiting the arrival of snow. However, the first kiss of the winter from King Frost, was to be later this year. It was already the 9th of December, and this year he was not due to give his frosty kiss until the 13th. If, however, you believed in a year of bad luck, then there were still several days left which, theoretically, could mean more bad luck.

King Frost had two very mischievous children, and it was also 1946. It was one of the years when the 13th day of December was on a Friday, which made most people nervous.

Due to the year's unusual circumstances, there was an emergency meeting of the council and a special meeting of the trustees who put some emergency measures into place, just in case they were needed.

No one knew what, if anything, would happen in those next few days but they were to be prepared for anything. The radio weather forecast said there was to be heavy snow for the Kingdom of Merry, but it was a clear blue sky and there were still butterflies in the gardens, more butterflies than had ever been seen at that time of the year. Everyone knew that when the Merry-Kiss had been done no butterfly was safe.

"Did you know Hanna that when the wings of a butterfly get cold it can't fly until it has warmed them up in the sunshine!"

"I knew that," said James, putting out his tongue at Hanna.

Rosy ignored him, she knew what was coming…

…Heavy rain a week earlier had brought with it a deluge of frogs and the cottages next to the loch had to keep their doors closed. The old mill's water wheel turned mysteriously at strange times and the robins sat on the clotheslines watching the butterflies.

Rosy had been almost five years old at the time but she still remembered her mother saying that sometimes robins pulled the wings off butterflies and she had been so upset that she refused to draw a robin on her Christmas cards. She also remembered with great joy that was the year she met Princess Jaclyn and was introduced to Kara, the Shetland pony.

"A Shetland pony, how lovely," said Hanna.

"Shall we stop for a few minutes and have some lemonade and biscuits?" suggested Rosy.

Misbehaving Children

Sometimes, Rosy found it difficult to remember the details of her mother's stories because they were often mingled in with her own memories. How had her mother begun that story? King Frost, she thought... or rather, his naughty children.

...King Frost was like any other father, very proud of his children. Sometimes, however, he felt as if they had forgotten that they were Royalty, and as such they should behave a little bit better than other children. They should set a good example, but instead they constantly caused problems. If there was trouble anywhere in the kingdom, he knew that he could usually find them somewhere in the middle of it.

Rosy was aware of the twins looking at each other but didn't stop.

...It was not exactly the good behaviour people expected from Royal children. The King had run out of excuses for them and didn't know what to do or how to teach them to be more responsible. He had decided that he'd make some serious changes when Dame Nature came because now it was December which was his busiest time of the year.

He wished that Princess Jaclyn and Prince John were the kind of children who could help him. They were now almost eleven years old, but instead of helping him they gave him more work undoing their childish mistakes. Even now, he was thinking of what they would be getting up to next, when he should have been concentrating on writing his list. The list of all the jobs he still had to do before the Merry-Kiss. The Merry-Kiss was later this year which was just as well because his list was getting longer. He hadn't even started the invitations for the Countdown or the Merry-Kiss Ball.

Princess Jaclyn came wandering into the room and disturbed his thoughts: she was bored. King Frost took a deep breath and wished that he had the time to be bored.

He thought for a moment, then he asked her to sit down at his desk and he handed her a writing pad and pen.

"Sit there," he said, "and do your old father a favour. Help me with one of the most important jobs in the kingdom."

Before he could say another word, Prince John entered the room and Princess Jaclyn made a face at him. He answered her look by putting out his tongue.

King Frost continued…

"You can write out the invitations for the Countdown and for the Merry-Kiss Ball. You must imagine that you are in control of this year's arrangements and write out the complete list of invitations. Then, send them out to everyone in the kingdom. When that's been done, there's a list of the foods to choose from, so that you can decide on the dinner menu and give it to the cook. Do you think that will be too much work for you to do, Jaclyn? Maybe John could help you!"

"NO, I can manage, father," she replied, in a slightly raised voice, then turned and smirked at her brother who again put out his tongue.

This time, the King saw them in the mantle mirror and felt a little disappointed in them.

Jaclyn and John were twins and as such, the King had always thought that they were close. Now he wondered if perhaps he had been wrong.

He turned to Prince John and asked if he would be willing to help with the Merry-Kiss.

"Of course, father," he replied, "I am the eldest and it is only right that I have more responsibility than Jaclyn."

"If you can think of any ideas for the entertainment that would be wonderful. You could also plan the fireworks display," answered the King. He turned in time to catch the sly look that Prince John gave his sister and it made him so angry.

He decided that now was the time that they both be taught a lesson: he wasn't going to wait. His children would now be his priority.

The Merry-Kiss preparations could wait.

He had an idea, but it would take planning. First, he would have to speak to some friends.

He asked everyone he could think of for their help: they agreed that the children needed to understand the seriousness of their Royal duties.

Everyone knew that they were not bad children, on the contrary, but it was time that they had a sharp reminder that with their titles, came serious responsibilities. The responsibilities of a whole Kingdom, and with that in mind they were all happy to play their part.

The Importance of a List

Princess Jaclyn sat at her father's desk writing the list of names. She began with relatives and friends, then neighbours, staff, schoolteachers, shop keepers, delivery people, every person, and living creature, in the Kingdom of Merry.

The Merry-Kiss was her favourite time of the year, not only because it was hers and John's birthday but because people came from all over Merry Kingdom to help them celebrate the Merry-Kiss.

The Merry-Kiss was the official first day of winter, one of the oldest traditions still practiced by the Frost family. Her father, King Frost, would ride throughout the Kingdom of Merry and beyond, making sure that his sparkling white frost missed nothing.

Princess Jaclyn had watched her father perform the Merry-Kiss many times and was in awe at the stunning patterns he made. The windowpanes on the castle were her favourites, they were like frozen works of art, as were the windows of every house in the village of Lakeside.

The pretty cottages that lined the loch were the most beautiful. As the sun set in the evening, the loch looked as if there was a bright orange fire beneath its icy exterior and every cottage window held its sparkling reflection.

The more Jaclyn thought about it the more excited she became. John entered her mind, and she couldn't help wondering what job her father had given him. She was sure that it couldn't be as important as hers. At that moment, her thoughts were interrupted by a fanfare of trumpets which meant that the king was summoning everyone to the great hall. Jaclyn left her list and made her way, along the many corridors to see what all the noise was about. She knew that it must be urgent because the trumpeters did not play the Royal Fanfare unless.

The King was sitting on the great throne, awaiting the arrival of his councillors, with Prince John to his right. The king smiled at Princess Jaclyn as she entered the throne room and beckoned her to sit beside him patting the seat of her own beautifully beaded throne. She couldn't help wondering what this was all about and judging by the look of bewilderment on John's face, he didn't know either.

The councillors entered the room, and acknowledged the King, Prince John, and Princess Jaclyn with a formal bow, then they sat.
The fanfare played again and when the King arose from his throne, the room fell silent.

"I have asked you all here because I need your help. I am to travel north to meet with Grandfather Frost, and I will be leaving immediately. Prince John and Princess Jaclyn will NOT be accompanying me. I know that they are not yet turned eleven, but I have decided that it is time for them to step in and perform some Royal duties. They will work together whilst I'm gone and share equally the preliminary duties for the Merry-Kiss. I would like you, my Council of Elders, to give your guidance to the Prince and Princess, should it be required. I would also like your blessings in passing to them the magic of Old Zero. Is there anyone present, against my wishes?"

The Princess expected a loud response, because she and John were not exactly in the good books of the members of the Council. They were not old enough to be given such responsibility, and still had several years of training ahead of them. They had many things to learn and had not even begun being schooled in the art of frost design, but the Council of Elders remained silent.

John and Jaclyn looked at each other, not believing what was happening.

"Very well then," said the King looking at his Councillors.

"Let it be written that today, Monday the 9th of December 1946, I bestowed to Prince John and

Princess Jaclyn a smidgen of the magic of Old Zero Frost, and they will perform the preliminary duties of the Merry-Kiss in my absence."

He paused for a moment then continued…

"I will return on Thursday the 12th of December to perform The Kiss. At five past midnight into Friday the 13th, we will have the Fireworks and the Birthday Honours, then we can begin the Merry-Kiss Ball."

He turned to look first at John and then at Jaclyn before saying…

"I cannot stress to you enough the importance of this work and want you to remember above all else, this: -

You must first think of the good name of Frost.

You must be loyal to your subjects, and respectful of every living creature.

You must protect every subject, human or creature, living within the Kingdom of Merry.

Do you understand and agree to this?"

John and Jaclyn nodded.

"Very well then," he said, "I will give each of you my blessing and with that will come some of the magic of Old Zero Frost. You will, however, not use any of the magical touch of Old Zero, until after I have performed the Kiss. Frost must only appear before your cousin Snow arrives, and she is not arriving until the 15th. So, there is to be no Pre-Merry-Kiss, do you understand me?"

Again, they nodded.

The King asked the Prince and Princess to stand in front of him, face each other and hold hands. As soon as they were in position, he moved his hands in a circular motion above their heads.

At first Princess Jaclyn didn't feel any different, then she had a cold tingling sensation throughout her body. She watched in amazement as the colour of John's eyes changed from sea green into a beautiful azure blue. His skin became pale, and his wayward, crazy, curly brown hair changed to the blueish white shade of an iceberg.

"Wow," she said aloud!

"Amazing," said John, who was staring at her with a look of disbelief.

She followed his gaze just in time to see the last of her long brown ringlets turn the same blueish white as Johns. She could hear her father still talking, but she didn't hear what he was saying, she just wanted to run to the nearest mirror and look at her pale skin, blue eyes, and her beautiful hair. She thought that if she looked anything like John, she must look so beautiful, but she wouldn't have said that to John.

Whilst King Frost was saying goodbye, he reminded them again of the importance of the work he had asked them to do and to make sure to double check all the invitations so as not to leave anyone out. He said that only once he had missed someone, and he had paid an extremely high price for that mistake.

To forget someone was the very highest insult. To be forgotten was to deny their very existence and they would therefore fade away, disappear from this world into the Aos Si.

"Where's That?"

"It's a place very close, but very far away, Hanna. The Aos Si is the world that runs parallel to ours. You'll find out more about it later in the story."

The king had looked so sad while he was talking, so Princess Jaclyn had assured him she would not forget anyone. She would ask John to double check the list for her. With that assurance the King gave each of them a hug and told them he would see them soon.

*

The following morning Princess Jaclyn went back to her father's study to continue writing out the list of invitations for the Countdown and the Merry-Kiss Ball. She knew that although she had agreed to do it, and was very happy to help her father, it was way more difficult than she had thought it would be. She knew that she needed help. Her father's list from the year before was no help at all because it was not up to date. Many of the invitations King Frost delivered personally were not on the list. She didn't want to ask any of the councillors for help because that would show them that she couldn't compile a simple list. She decided to swallow her pride and ask John, or rather ask his opinion as to how she could double check her list to make, absolutely, sure that she had invited everyone.

Her father's last words ran once again through her mind. *Remember, Do Not Forget Anyone, because to forget someone will deny their existence.* If she were to forget someone, she would pay a high price.

By the afternoon Jaclyn had finished the list and was searching the castle for John but couldn't find him anywhere. Just as she was about to give up, she found him next to the water fountain in the garden.

"Look Jaclyn, look!"

He said excitedly as she walked toward him.

"Have you ever seen anything so beautiful?"

Jaclyn looked at the large three-layered water fountain in the centre of the garden and realised that the bottom layer was sparkling.

"What have you done! You heard father; we're not supposed to freeze anything until the 13th. He will be furious if he finds out."

"Oh, Jaclyn, please... Stop with your I'm a little angel routine, it doesn't work with me. I know you're no angel, even if father doesn't. We must practice if we're going to help him with the Merry-Kiss. I don't know about you, but I want father to be proud of me and if that means that I practice a few days before, then I practice a few days before. Anyway, I've already finished all the jobs I had to do, including the layout of the fireworks: what do you want?"

"Defrost it immediately, before someone sees it," she shouted at him, then she walked away. She was so angry with him that she didn't ask for his help. She was convinced he wouldn't be able to help anyway.

As she gave the invitations to the footman for delivery, she had the strangest feeling, one of those deep down inside feelings, when you just know that something isn't right. She had gone over the list a hundred times and everyone seemed to be accounted for so she decided that instead of wasting more time worrying about it, she would get on with choosing the food for the menu.

All the ingredients had to be ordered and there were only a few days left until the Ball.

Her father had really left everything right to the last minute this year, which wasn't like him at all, but then she thought it had really been a strange kind of year. It had always been the job of her mother to keep her father's agenda on track. Now that he was having to organise everything himself, he wasn't doing a very good job of it, which could be why Grandfather Frost wanted to see him.

The menus, and the ordering of the food took priority in her mind and the list of names was forgotten. Her mind was now in the land of imagination fantasising that had she been given the task sooner, she could have made it a masked Ball, or a masquerade, but it was way too late. However, she made several notes for the future. She was really enjoying this responsibility and fully intended to ask her father if she could plan the Ball every year.

She glanced at herself in the mirror in her father's study, trying to get used to her new look. She didn't want to be vain, but she really thought that it was her father's most beautiful work to date. How amazing she would have looked if it had been a masquerade Ball. She thought of John and decided she'd better go and see what he was up to. Although, if he was up to no good, she didn't want to know. She didn't want half of whatever he was going to get when her father got back and found out what he'd been up to.

The image of the water fountain came into her head, and she had to admit to herself that it did look pretty impressive for his first time at freezing something. She couldn't help but wonder if hers would be as good. She looked out of the study window in time to see John heading down the road toward the loch. Oh dear, she thought, this isn't going to end well, maybe I should follow him and see what he's up to.

It's Magic

John half ran and half danced skipping on and off the pavement at the side of the winding road toward the village. He had totally forgotten his new hair colour and how different his appearance was. Everyone that he met on his way stared at him and by the time he was halfway down the hill he had a following of frogs, robins, and noisy children, in that order. The frogs and robins were there by special invitation, but the children were not.

It was obvious that they didn't recognise him which, after a few moments of thought he decided, could work in his favour. If no one knew who he was, how could he be blamed if his plan should go wrong. He didn't have Jaclyn there to take half of the blame and he knew that she wouldn't approve of what he had in his mind, but..., a crafty grin crossed his lips as he created a picture in his mind.

"Shoo children, go on shoo," he shouted.

"Go away and stop following me or I'll turn you all into frogs like I did to the others," pointing to the trail of frogs behind him.

The children looked at all the frogs, screamed, and ran in different directions leaving John laughing hysterically.

He continued walking until he came to the fork in the road at the first cottage then he turned toward the old watermill. He looked around to make sure no one was there, then he whistled on the frogs to gather around him.

The wheel of the watermill creaked and groaned and began to turn. John thought he heard someone, but he saw no one, only the frogs that were now jumping off the rotating water wheel into the loch.
While he watched the frogs, his mind was thinking about what job he could get the robins to do for the Merry-Kiss, but since he couldn't think of anything at that moment, he sent them all home.

As he looked over at the rotating wheel of the watermill, he realised that he had never seen the wheel turn before and was wishing Jaclyn had been there to see it. Jaclyn always had opinions on why strange things happened.

He stared into the loch as if waiting for inspiration then, he put one finger onto the surface of the water, moved it around and around, then back and forth in different directions. It was as if he was writing and drawing all at the same time. The water got colder, and he saw the most amazing frosty designs begin to appear on the surface. He had never seen anything like it, not even his father had made something quite so unique.

He turned to the frogs.

"Did you see that?" He asked them.

Remember that pattern, because one day, when I am king, you will all be helping me with the Merry-Kiss.
The frogs hopped onto the thin ice to examine the intricate patterns.

As John stood watching the frogs admire his work, he had the strangest feeling. He could imagine that this must be the feeling his father had when he stood before all his subjects. As he looked at all the frogs, he stood tall and made his very first proclamation ... but without the trumpeting fanfare.

"I Prince John, have decided that I am going to give you, my trusted frogs, a small amount of the gift of Old Zero, so that every time you hop onto something you will create a beautiful frosty pattern."

The frogs were ecstatic, they began hopping up and down in anticipation. They had never been asked to do anything quite so important before.
As John watched them huddle together on the frozen patch of loch, he had one of his brainwaves.
Maybe I can save some time by stirring the water with them all huddled together, that means that they

will all receive the power at the same time. If I do it one at a time, I'll be here all night.

He decided that was his greatest idea so far and his finger broke the thin layer of frost on the loch's surface.

As he began drawing in circles he declared:

"I Prince John, give each frog a frizzle of the power of Old Zero. However, in passing to you this honour, I must ask each of you to promise Not to use the power until after my father performs the Merry-Kiss!"

The frogs nodded their agreement and John continued.

"The Merry-Kiss is only two days away and we must all work together to make it the best ever."

As John continued to turn his finger around in the water, the surface of the loch began to sparkle with the frosty crystals. The frogs shivered and looked around.

Frogs don't like to be cold, and John was so busy enjoying himself making patterns that he didn't notice them disappear down into the mud to keep warm.

By the time he noticed they were gone it was dark: he assumed they had gone home so he headed back to the castle.

He kept thinking how proud his father was going to be.

Unlucky for One

It was Wednesday the 11 of December 1946.

The palace had been a hive of activity all day. The servants had all been cleaning, polishing, and carrying tables and chairs into the large ballroom. Beautiful sparkling blue decorations had been hung over all the archways and doors along the corridors leading to the great hall, all in preparation for the Merry-Kiss Ball.

The Kiss was to begin at one minute past midnight as the 12th changed into Friday the 13th. King Frost would be back in time to do the official countdown.

The Ball would begin, right after the first kiss of frost was complete.

The coming year was hopefully going to be a special one. A Merry-Kiss beginning on Friday the 13th was always a good one and was usually followed by a blessed and fruitful year.

Prince John and Princess Jaclyn were busy directing the servants as to what decorations went where and continually checking their lists to make sure all would be in place for the countdown when suddenly they heard a scream and the sound of breaking glass, from the ballroom.

John and Jaclyn along with several servants went running. One of the maids was staring, pale faced, out of the large ballroom window at the water fountain.

A minute before it had been free flowing, but it was now frozen solid.

The rose garden glistened with a frosty white and there were several butterflies frozen onto the waterspouts of the fountain.

Princess Jaclyn gasped and covered her mouth with her hand.

"Oh John," she whispered, "what have you done?"

"WAIT Rosy! John couldn't have done it!" shouted James.

"I'm sure he didn't do it, Rosy, it's probably the bad luck working again," cried Hanna. "Oh, those poor butterflies."

"Don't worry Hanna... they'll be fine," said Rosy.

John turned to Jaclyn, "I've done nothing, how could I have done that when I've been right here beside you this whole time."

He turned and ran out into the garden closely followed by Jaclyn. Together they searched looking for any clue as to who the culprit might have been. John knew that it hadn't been him and if it wasn't Jaclyn, then it had to have been one of the frogs.

However, there were no frogs in the garden and apart from the frozen fountain there was no sign that a frog had ever been there. John still had to go and talk to them just in case.

He set off for the loch accompanied by Jaclyn, who wasn't going to let him out of her sight until she found out who else had the ability to freeze.
On the way he confessed to her what he had organised with the frogs and whilst Jaclyn could see the logic of it, she knew that her father would be very angry.

By the time they arrived at the loch it was dark, and they were finding it difficult to see because there were no lights on in any of the nearby cottages and the moon was covered by clouds.

When John whistled and called out to the frogs, a light came on in one of the cottages which cast a bright glow over the loch.

Jaclyn gasped in horror.

The loch was just as frozen as the water fountain. Every bush and tree near the watermill sparkled.

"Oh John!" Jaclyn said, in a frantic voice.

"I did not do that!" Exclaimed John emphatically.

"I only gave the surface of the loch a small frosting as a demonstration, but it had thawed before I left. It really did Jaclyn, you have to believe me, I didn't do this."

Jaclyn looked at her brother's worried face and knew that he was telling the truth, but she also knew that her father was never going to believe him.
Her mind was racing trying to think of what they could do to make things right. They did not yet have the ability to defrost something so large.

The Merry-Kiss was getting closer, everyone would be arriving the next day for the countdown.

There was a rustle from some nearby bushes and a frog hopped out.

"Did you do this to the loch and to the trees," demanded John?

"Oh No Sir, not me Sir, I didn't do it, I don't know how to freeze things!" croaked the frog.

"I received my invitation for the Merry-Kiss, and came early to find my family and friends, but I can't find them anywhere. After the loch froze over, I was so cold I tried to find some warm mud, then I heard you talking."

"When did you arrive?" asked Jaclyn?

"Just after the sun went down, a few moments before the loch froze over."

"Didn't you see anyone?" asked a puzzled John.

"No Sir, no one," croaked the frog.

Jaclyn thanked the frog and told him to go to the castle and get a warm meal.

"Tell the servants that I, Princess Jaclyn, sent you, and that you are one of my special guests."

Until that moment the frog had no idea to whom he was talking. He cleared his throat and bowed low.

"I'm so sorry your Majesties, I didn't recognise you."

"Understandable," said Prince John, "oh and please don't tell anyone about what you've seen here, I mean the frozen loch and the trees."

The frog assured them he wouldn't tell anyone and hopped away toward the castle to get warm.

John began telling Jaclyn about the mill wheel turning the day before and how strange it was. He asked her if she had ever seen it turn before. She said that she thought it was broken and had been for many years, but, before leaving, they gave the room above the watermill a thorough search.

As they walked home, they were no wiser as to who could have done it or what could have happened but decided that they would return, at first light, the next day. They were going to need a lot of help to thaw out all the ice. There had to be no sign of frost by the afternoon because that's when the first of the guests were due to arrive.

*

By the time they got home the servants had defrosted the fountain and John posted guards to make sure it wouldn't happen again. Sadly, there was nothing he could do about the butterflies. He lifted them carefully and took them into the glass house. In the morning they'd be facing the morning sun, he thought, and perhaps if they thawed out slowly, they'd come back to life.

He wished that Mother Nature had been there because she would have known what to do. One touch from her would bring them the breath of life.

A feeling of great sadness came over him. He felt ashamed that he could not have protected the poor butterflies.

Who could have done such a thing, he thought?

Always Ask for Help

When John and Jaclyn arrived at the loch, early the next morning, Mrs Achaius was already there, looking very confused as she tapped at the ice on the surface of the loch.

John and Jaclyn knew all the people who lived in the houses by the loch because they were the King's trustees. John thought that perhaps Mrs Achaius, or one of the others, had seen something.

When he and Jaclyn arrived at the gate of the first cottage, he saw a girl playing in the garden.

"Oh, I remember this bit, that's Rosy, isn't it?" Hanna asked, excitedly?

Rosy smiled and nodded...

The little girl smiled at him and asked Jaclyn if they were in fancy dress for the Ball at the castle. John had forgotten about how different they both looked.

Jaclyn smiled and told the girl they were going to a birthday party.

"Oh, that's nice," said the girl, "it's my birthday tomorrow."

"Ours too," replied Princess Jaclyn, smiling.

The girl smiled back and called for her mother to come.
Mrs Achaius stepped back from the loch and gave them a welcoming smile.
As she approached the gate, not recognising them, she asked who they were and could she help them.

John and Jaclyn smiled, and Mrs Achaius was given a quick introduction to their new look.

John asked her if she had noticed anything strange happening around dusk, at the loch, the day before.

"Come into the house and I'll make us a warm drink. It'll be warmer than standing here," she replied: so, they followed her into the house.

"Now then," she smiled, handing them each a cup of hot chocolate, "what's all this about and how can I help?"

Just as Prince John was about to speak, she handed her daughter Rosy an apple.

"Can I keep it to give to the horse," she asked?

"What kind of horse do you have, Rosy," asked John smiling at her?

"We don't have a horse," interrupted Mrs Achaius, "Rosy's talking about your father's horse."

John and Jaclyn just stared at each other.

"I'll show you where it lives if you like?" said Rosy, running toward the door.

They followed her out into the garden.

"Over there," she said, pointing to the mill.

"It lives over there."

John and Jaclyn glanced at each other and smiled, because Rosy pointing to the mill confirmed what they had been thinking. They now knew 'who', or rather 'what', had been responsible for everything that had been happening. However, they also knew that they had to take full responsibility, because they were the ones to be blamed. Fortunately, it was still pre-Merry-Kiss, so it wasn't too late to try and put things right before their father arrived back, but first they had to find a way to defrost the ice on the loch.

They went back into the cottage and Jaclyn asked Mrs Achaius if she had a pen and some paper. John asked her if she could think of any way of defrosting the loch before all the guests began arriving. Mrs Achaius understood completely why it was so important that the frost on the loch be gone as soon as possible. She made several telephone calls to the other trustees and explained the situation.

By the time the trustees arrived she had an idea. She explained the quickest way to defrost the ice.

The water in our taps is cold, but the ice is colder, so if you open your garden hoses and direct the spouts onto the loch it should melt the ice enough for it to break; then we can remove the pieces.
The trustees agreed and they left to put the plan into action.

The trees and bushes had already thawed in the sun but the thick layer of ice on the loch was going to take much longer.

They watched in wonder as the seven spouts of water skooshed into the air and land onto the loch.

It wasn't long until the ice began melting, enough for the hammers to break through.

Three sturdy boats dragging heavy nets sailed across the loch, back and forth, until every piece of ice had been removed.

As soon as the loch was ice free, Prince John and Princess Jaclyn gave a huge sigh of relief. They thanked them for their help and understanding and apologised for the mayhem they had caused by their stupid actions.

They thanked Mrs Achaius and Rosy, then headed toward the watermill.

They sat on the wall at the side of the mill and waited until the sun went down, then John whistled.

The frogs appeared from under the mud and hopped onto the wheel of the mill. John began apologising to them, but the frogs didn't know what he was talking about because they had been fast asleep under the warm mud.

He asked them once again to huddle together and he put his finger into the loch and turned it around in circles, but this time he reversed the magic and took back the power of Old Zero.

He thanked all the frogs for their help and told them their cousin was at the castle waiting for them, and to go and get ready for the Merry-Kiss.

They watched the frogs hopping up the road toward the castle, then turned their attention onto the watermill.

John whistled as loud as he could, and the large waterwheel began to turn.

"If only it had been turning like that before, the loch might not have frozen so easily," said Jaclyn.

John nodded and whistled again.

The water under the mill wheel began to bubble.

They jumped back from the edge just in time as a spectacular pure white Neugle leaped out of the loch onto the land at the side of them.

"Wow" ...shouted James, "a white one."

A Neugle Forgotten

Shem bowed low in honour of the Prince and Princess and waited to see what his punishment was going to be.

"Hello Shem," said Prince John, "how are you? My sister and I have something we wish to talk to you about."

First, he apologised for the noise of the hammers on the loch but explained that there was no other way to remove the ice.

Shem nodded.

"Do you have something to tell us, Shem?" asked John.

Shem looked at the serious looking faces of the Prince and the Princess and was about to dive into the safety of the water when he felt a sudden burst of courage.

"I beg for your pardon Prince John, but it was not my fault that you gave me some of Old Zero's magic. I thought that since I had not received my invitation to the Merry-Kiss, King Frost had forgotten me. I did not wish to cease to exist in this world and thought if only I could help, it would be a tribute to King Frost and perhaps he would give me an invitation to join the countdown."

Shem slowly began to relate the events that had taken place…

First, he reminded them of how he had lived at the mill for as long as he could remember. How he had believed that he was one of the king's closest friends and how the King normally visited him every day. How the King had always made him feel as if he belonged, as if he were one of the family.
However, he hadn't seen him for several days and assumed that he had forgotten him. The thought of that had made him feel very sad. King Frost had never missed giving him his invitation to the Merry-Kiss; but this year everyone had received their invitation, except him.

He felt even more sad because he knew that he would soon fade away, no longer exist, then something strange happened...

He heard someone whistle, so he swam up to the mill wheel to see who it could be...

The whistle sounded familiar, and he thought that King Frost had come to deliver his invitation in person, however… it wasn't King Frost.

He explained how he had hidden in the bushes at the side of the loch because from there he could get a better view of what was going on. The whistler was Prince John, he was talking to some of the frogs. He was showing them how to make all the beautiful patterns with frost on the loch.

Oh, if only Prince John could teach him to make those kinds of patterns, he thought, he would have a job to do, and he'd be needed.

The very thought of that had made him feel so happy and as he listened to Prince John, he decided that, like the frogs, that he would help Prince John with the Merry-Kiss. So, he changed himself into a frog and slipped back into the water just in time for the Prince to pass on the magic of old Zero to all the frogs.

When the Prince had gone and all the frogs were snuggled together, fast asleep, under the warm mud he changed back into himself.

He thought long and hard if he should use the power or not. No punishment could be worse that what was about to happen to him, but he decided he'd sleep on it and see if he thought the same the next day.

The next afternoon he had made his decision and set off to test his new power. He couldn't wait to get a glimpse of the patterns of frost he would be able to make.

Although he didn't have fingers like Prince John or the frogs, he did have a round wheel like tail that he could unwind when he wanted to reach something far away or high up, and he had four hooves which meant that he could travel faster than the frogs... and jump higher. Or he could simply change himself into a whatever.

"But I asked you not to use the power before the Merry-Kiss!" Exclaimed John.

"And as a frog I didn't."

"Very clever," Jaclyn said, smiling at Shem.

Shem continued...

The first place he could think of to test his power was the water fountain in the palace gardens because he knew he couldn't touch the loch.

It was still early evening when he arrived.

He changed the colour of his coat from arctic white to a mixture of greens so that no one would see him in the garden. He hadn't felt so much excitement in years, and the best part was no one knew that he had some of Old Zero's magic. He could really let himself go and have some fun.

He gave the Princess a little smile and continued...

At first, he wasn't sure how to do it, then he

remembered that John had made circles in the water
with his finger. He reared up in front of the water
fountain and uncurled his tail. He swished the water
back and forth on each level of the fountain and as
he curled and uncurled his tail it hit the water on
each level. By the time he was finished the fountain
looked like a beautiful ice carving.
He was busy admiring his workmanship when he
heard one of the maids scream and saw faces at the
castle windows, so he left.

As he galloped down the road toward home, his tail
flicked the leaves of the occasional tree or bush by
the roadside. He felt so happy.

As he entered the loch at the side of the mill's
waterwheel, he sneezed.

When a Neugle sneezes no matter how hard they try
they can't stop their tail from uncurling. He had
tried so hard to curl it up without splashing the
water, but he couldn't, and when his tail hit the
loch…

"All the water began to freeze," Prince John added.

Shem said he had only just managed to get under the
waterwheel before the whole surface of the loch was
frozen over.

He hadn't meant to freeze the loch but the fact that it
was now frozen meant that he and the frogs, like it or

not, were stuck under the ice with no way out until it melted.

The more he had thought about it the worse he felt.

He knew that King Frost was sure to be angry with him because it was King Frost who performed the Merry-Kiss and now that he, Shem, had frozen the fountain and the loch there could be no countdown because it had already been done. King Frost was his best friend and he had let him down.

He had thought and thought of what he could do to make things right before it was too late, but what could he do when there was no way for him to get out of the loch. He couldn't change whilst he was in the water.

He had just settled himself into his misery when he heard, what he thought was, someone knocking. He looked up in time to see a huge object hit the ice, then another and another and saw the cracks appearing all over the loch. He saw the trustees removing the chunks of ice and loading it into their boats and he thought of helping but how, it was still daylight.

Then just as daylight began to fade, he heard the Prince's whistle.

Princess Jaclyn had been listening very carefully and felt so bad because she knew that his invitation had been her responsibility. It was her fault as well as John's.

She lifted Shem's face into her hands and looking into his lovely eyes took a deep breath...

"It was I who forgot you Shem, not my father. Please forgive me, I really am so sorry."

She told him that it was she who had been given the task of writing the invitations and although she had a feeling, she had missed someone, because of her pride she had not asked her brother or the Councillors to check her list. She had not meant to leave him out and she was deeply sorry.

"We also know that John should not have been using the power before the Merry-Kiss. You are in no way to blame for anything that has happened. Can you please forgive my brother and I for our selfish actions and our lack of care for your feelings?"

Shem rolled out his tail, curled it around them and they all hugged.

"Thank you, Shem," said a relieved Jaclyn.

"Now, if you're in agreement, I'd like to pay you a small honour, so that it will act as a reminder and never again will you be forgotten."

John glanced at his sister wondering what she was going to do.

Princess Jaclyn smiled at Shem and rubbed his nose affectionately.

"I promise you that this old mill will be renewed as soon as possible, and it will be renamed 'Neugle' mill."

"Oh, Your Highnesses," cried Shem, "I'm not worthy of such an honour."

"You are indeed worthy," said Prince John.

"Even when you thought everyone had forgotten you and you were about to fade from existence, your only thought was to help my father with the Merry-Kiss. I will speak with my father and try to find something for you to do that will keep you busy when my father is on a trip. I promise you that one day, when I am king, you will help me with the Merry-Kiss. I saw what you did to the fountain in the garden, and it was truly magnificent."

Jaclyn smiled at her brother and nodded her agreement. She put her hand into her cloak pocket and took out of it a very special handwritten invitation and handed it to Shem.

Shem thanked her, bowed even lower than before, wished them farewell until later: then he disappeared into the loch with a splash.

Mrs Achaius was still busy emptying buckets of ice into the well in the garden when she heard Rosy shouting goodbye.

The Merry-Kiss

It was twenty minutes before midnight and the castle grounds were crowded, everyone eagerly awaiting the balcony appearance of King Frost.

Jaclyn went over her list again as she waited outside the balcony doors.

Grand fanfare from the trumpeters.

Father's appearance on the balcony.

Father's short speech.

The countdown

The Kiss.

The Birthday Honours

Father's signal to light the fireworks.

Sign to the orchestra to play the father daughter dance to start the Ball.

Well. that was how it normally went, but nothing this year was normal, and everyone would sigh a breath of relief when the year of bad luck was finally over.

King Frost had still not arrived, and she was getting worried...

"Oh, I hope nothing bad has happened to him," Hanna said, looking worried.

John began wondering what his father would do if he were in his position. ... what would he do?

The Merry-Kiss had to go ahead at midnight no matter what.

*

The castle grounds were beautiful.

The water in the fountain flashed beautiful colours in time with the music and the twinkling of the garden lights.

Some of the youngsters were becoming restless and John was trying to keep them amused.

Jaclyn thought that he looked quite grown up in his silver suit and his azure satin bow tie. She had chosen the fabric to match her father's and this year's Merry-Kiss colours. Her gown had a wide azure coloured sash, the same as John's bow tie.

John caught her looking at him and smiled with a kindness, she had never seen from him before.

John was thinking how Jaclyn looked so grown up, and how she was becoming so wise. He also thought, that one day, she would make an amazing Queen.
He knew that he had many years of growing up still to do before he could reach her level, but that was okay because he knew that she'd push him along the right path, and meanwhile, he could still have adventures.

*

It was five minutes before midnight and John and Jaclyn were waiting outside the balcony doors.

The king had still not arrived, and they looked at each other not knowing what to do. Suddenly, John had an idea and whispered it into Jaclyn's ear. She smiled at him and nodded, then he turned and walked briskly off along the corridor.

Jaclyn waved to the trumpeters to start the fanfare. The fanfare would normally have been the lead up to her father's balcony appearance.

The trumpeters gave a wonderful performance and as they finished Jaclyn took a deep breath and stepped onto the balcony.

As she looked down at the crowd below, she saw so many familiar faces and realised something. All these guests were not just guests, no, they were not guests, they were so much more.

She smiled and waved to the crowd, then she began…

"Welcome to all of you, our dearest family…"
"Thank you so much for coming to join in with the countdown to this year's Merry-Kiss."

"Before we begin the countdown, I want to take the time to thank all of you, for the love and kindness that you have shown my brother and I during my father's absence. The help that you gave to us in our hour of need was done with love and kindness and for that we will be eternally grateful. Until now, I don't think that Prince John nor I fully appreciated the love and kindness that you give to us each day, and for that, we give you all our sincerest apologies. We took you all for granted, thinking of you merely as my father's guests, friends, neighbours, or subjects. However, these last few days have shown us that you are so much more than that… you are all our dearest family."

There was a loud cheering and applause from the crowd and Jaclyn continued…

"Tonight, instead of my father, Prince John and I, with the help of some of our very talented 'family,' are going to perform for you our very first Merry-

Kiss. I'm sure you will find it very different, but we hope that you will all enjoy it!"

Jaclyn expected a response but there was silence.

She continued...

"I have it on good authority that our year of bad luck has come to an end and that this coming year is going to be a very special one. This year our Merry-Kiss day starts on Friday the 13th and although I've heard it described as 'unlucky for some' thankfully the 'some' does not apply to us."

The cheers were so loud that the people almost missed Jaclyn begin the countdown ..."10, 9, 8, 7... "

Jaclyn hadn't been aware of John on the balcony until she heard him join in the countdown. She felt him take her hand and when they reached zero, they leaned over the balcony and each blew a kiss of frost into the air.

Some of the people were visibly shivering watching the beautiful tiny crystals floating down toward them.

On cue from John the orchestra leader tapped his wand on the stand and music filled the air.

The waterspouts of the fountain pushed out the water in time to the music, and when Shem tapped them with his tail, they froze into miniature waterfalls. The crowd cheered so loud it was deafening.

Some of the children standing next to the small pond in the garden began to cheer and people ran to see what was happening.

The frogs were hopping all over the pond making the most beautiful sparkling frosty designs and the lily pads looked like little silver boats sailing all over the pond.

Some of the frogs were leaping from side to side touching the plants and bushes, each touch frostier than the last until the bushes looked as if they were wearing sparkling white gowns.

John and Jaclyn looked as if they were floating as they gave the kiss of frost to each tree, plant, and window in and around the castle.

Shem went back to the loch to perform a very special frosty kiss so that the ice was thick enough for the children to skate on the next day. He wasn't worried that he would not be able to hide in the water until the big thaw came because he knew he could now sleep peacefully in Neugle mill.

Jaclyn smiled at her brother and hugged him as she congratulated him on his best idea ever.

"I'll second that!" exclaimed the King, stepping out from behind the large oak next to the fountain.

John was shocked to see his father. He expected, at the very least, a lecture, however...

"This Merry-Kiss is one of the best I've ever seen." King Frost continued. "I'm so proud of you both. I truly thought I'd have to show myself when Shem froze the loch, but you acted so quickly in having the ice removed, it wasn't necessary. Then tonight when I didn't arrive, you took over John, and Jaclyn, I was amazed at your speech, it was very moving. I'm happy to see how close you have become. You have proven to me that one day, you will make a wonderful king and queen. Now, there is something I must do and then, my beautiful daughter, I will be expecting the first dance with you to begin this year's Ball."

Jaclyn and John hugged their father, then John waved to someone at the other side of the garden. There was a loud crack as a firework exploded in the sky and the sky lit up in a rainbow of colours, then another crack, and another, until the whole sky looked as if it was full of exploding stars falling to the earth.

While the crowd watched the fireworks and sung Happy Birthday, Shem arrived to let John know that the loch was thick enough for the children to skate on.

As they watched the sky light up with all the different coloured fireworks, they heard a whinny close by and they turned to see the King walking toward them with a beautiful white Shetland pony.

"I'd like to introduce you all to the new addition to our family," he said.

"This is Kara."

"When I heard that she was the last of her kind and that she was alone on the Island of Hoy, I went to ask her if she would like to come and live with us. She had heard so many stories about neugles that she was especially excited to meet you Shem."

Shem could hardly believe what he was seeing, Kara was so beautiful.

"If you don't mind Shem, I still have many things to do tonight so, I will leave you and Kara to get acquainted," and he passed Kara's reigns to Wellan, a stable boy at the castle.

Shem nodded and bowed his head.

The King entered the hall to great cheers from the crowd.

There was an even louder cheer and applause as the Prince and Princess entered.

The King nodded to the orchestra and took his daughter by the hand.

As they walked to the middle of the dance floor Jaclyn glanced back at John who was leading Rosy by the hand toward them.

"Oh... that's so nice," said Hanna.

"Yes...it is...and I'm really glad they didn't get into trouble," James added.

Rosy's Red Cheeks

The night of the first Merry-Kiss performed by Prince John and Princess Jaclyn had been one that no one would ever forget. Especially Rosy because it had all happened on her sixth birthday. When you're young you can sometimes think that the wonderful things that happen on your birthday are meant only for you... and thinking back on it, she could understand why....

It was 13 December 1946 and Rosy had now been six years old for a whole five minutes. Whilst she and her mother stood with all the other guests watching the fireworks display in the castle gardens. Rosy imagined that the most spectacular of all the fireworks were a birthday gift just for her. A tap on her shoulder made her turn very fast and there before her was Princess Jaclyn. She was wearing the most beautiful party dress Rosy had ever seen.

"It's Rosy isn't it, your name I mean?"
Rosy was still looking at her dress, mesmerised by the sparkling crystals all over the azure blue sash. She smiled and nodded.

"I didn't get the chance to really thank you for telling us about... em... the King's horse, and I remembered you saying that it was your birthday today!"

Rosy nodded again and then added, "And it's your birthday too and your brothers, Happy Birthday."

"Thank you Rosy, but tonight, as a special thank you for all your help, we have a birthday surprise for you."

Rosy was now beaming, she didn't know what to say, she looked up at her mother, who nodded her approval. Rosy would never have thought a Princess would give 'Her' a birthday gift.

"I'd like you to meet Shem, my father's horse, and this is Shem's friend Kara."

Rosy turned to see Prince John walking toward them with Wellan, one of the stable boys, who was holding the lead reigns of Shem and a horse she had never seen before.

"Happy Birthday, Prince John," she called out shyly.

She knew Shem very well, but she didn't tell them that. She saw Shem's eyes bright and flashing green with love and happiness.

"Kara has granted you permission to ride her, but Rosy, you are only to ride her when your mother is with you, at least until you learn to ride and are a little bit older." Prince John said awkwardly.

Rosy was ecstatic. She felt like she had been given her very own horse to keep, and Kara was so beautiful. She was as white as snow, with blue eyes and an amazing soft wispy mane that fell in ringlets to her knees. Her thick bushy tail didn't look anything like Shem's, hers was far too short to curl around like a wheel.

"Wait... stop... stop... if the King's horse, Shem, is a Neugle," asked Hanna, "then how can he ride him and be able to get back off?"

Before Rosy could answer, James said, "Just because he's the King's horse Hanna, doesn't mean he rides him. Maybe if people know that Shem is the Kings horse, they won't try to ride him so it will protect him."

"Oh, of course, I didn't think of that."

Rosy smiled, noticing how nice they were being to each other and continued with the story.

...Rosy, gently, and lovingly, rubbed Kara's nose and smiled, then turned to Shem. She had looked into Shem's eyes many times when feeding him with carrots and apples and had always felt a great trust. Now as she looked into his green eyes, she saw more than trust and she knew she had his approval to her friendship with Kara.

"Come on Rosy let's go into the ballroom it's almost time."

Rosy took the hand of Princess Jaclyn and they ran toward the ballroom, Prince John trying to keep up with them.

King Frost saw the arrival of his daughter and held out his hand for their father daughter dance.

Jaclyn smiled pleadingly at her brother and asked, "John will you dance with Rosy, for her birthday?"

John hated dancing and she knew that, but tonight, he would dismiss his dislikes, he was so happy.

He smiled down at Rosy and held out his hand.

The music began, and Rosy blushed as she took his hand. She had only ever danced with her mother. She had never held any boys hand before, never mind the hand of a Prince. She giggled when he asked her to try and not step on the toes of his new shoes.

Rosy fell asleep that night with a feeling of such happiness. It was a happiness greater than she had ever known. She believed that she would awaken in the morning and find out that it had all been a dream. However, a dream it was not, and the next morning she awoke to find a beautiful white riding outfit, boots, and hat on the chair in her room. She dressed quickly and ran downstairs.

Her mother was sitting at the kitchen table drinking her tea, she beamed the biggest smile toward her when she walked in, wearing her new riding outfit.

"It's for your birthday," her mother smiled.

"This morning we're going to the stables. You can have your first riding lesson, then after you've changed out of those new clothes, I'll teach you how to groom Kara and Shem. As my mother always say's, you're never too young to learn. Mind you, we might have to find a soapbox for you to stand on so you're tall enough," and she laughed.

Rosy took to riding as if she had been born in the saddle of a horse and she had the most wonderful day.

*

In the weeks, months, and years that followed, Rosy learned to ride Kara like a true champion.

The Letter

In June 1951, Rosy left the Lakeside village school. After the summer holidays she began the new term at her senior school. It took almost an hour to get to Drallon on the bus, but it was nearer than the two-hour trip to the city.

She had never had much homework in primary school, but now her homework began to take up most of her free time. She never seemed to have a moment to herself, and hardly ever went to the stables. She really began to feel the strain of all the schoolwork, and sadness filled most of her days.

The Christmas holidays, and the yearly Merry-Kiss, were a consolation, but she lived in dread at the thought of going back when the holidays were over.

Her days at school felt never ending.

She was missing Shem and Kara so much that it began to weigh heavily on her heart, and she walked around the school under a cloud of sadness. However, on Wednesday the 6 of February 1952, when most of her classmates were upset at the passing of the King, at his Estate in England. No matter how hard she tried she just couldn't feel sad. All she could think of was how happy she was at being sent home and having no school for a whole week.

On another occasion, she cried so much that her mother had to keep her off from school and take her to the stables.

When she saw how happy Shem and Kara were to see her, she felt much better and spent the rest of her day riding Kara, talking to Shem, and brushing them.

On some of her other sad days, her mother would comfort her by telling her that it would soon be the weekend, or it would soon be the Easter holidays.
Her education was important, and she knew that, but she missed Shem and Kara so much.

The summer holidays were her second favourite time of the year, when she had a whole eight weeks to spend with her mother in the garden; a whole eight weeks of riding Kara, and not a bit of homework.
It wasn't that she found her schoolwork difficult, she just had so much of it.

*

One evening when she was in the stable getting Shem ready, the King and Princess Jaclyn arrived. She was so happy to see Jaclyn, and the Princess hugged her warmly. Princess Jaclyn was home schooled and missed the company of another female. Although she was five years older than Rosy, they enjoyed being in each other's company. They chatted about favourite things to do, clothes, places, and of course, school. In fact, they were so wrapped up in their conversation, they didn't notice the King leave.

When the King arrived back, he told Rosy that her mother wanted to see her. Rosy hugged Jaclyn goodbye, and they arranged to meet the following day to go for a ride.

When Rosy arrived home, her mother was in the living-room reading a letter. She had tears rolling down her cheeks but when she saw Rosy, she smiled, then hugged her so tight Rosy could hardly breathe.

"I've had some really important news," she said excitedly.

"I'm going to have to leave you for a month, or maybe even longer. The King has very kindly offered that you go and live at the castle with them while I'm gone. You'll be happy to know that you don't have to travel to school anymore."

Rosy could feel a sadness tighten in her chest at the thought of her mother leaving her, they had never been apart before, but as the words 'no more traveling to school' reached her ears, happiness took over.

"No school?" she asked smiling.

"No traveling to school, Rosy. Of course, you will still have school, but it will be at the castle, with the tutor of the Princess and her brother."

Rosy was so excited, she could hardly wait to talk to Jaclyn the next day. She had completely forgotten about feeling sad that her mother was leaving.

*

That night, after her mother had packed their suitcases and given Rosy her instructions on what to do until her return, Rosy learned the real reason for her mother's sudden departure.

The letter had come from France.

"A man's been found that fits the description of your father. It seems that he was badly wounded during the war and got separated from his unit. No one knew who he was, and he couldn't tell them, because he couldn't remember anything. He was in hospital for a long time, and although he got better physically, he never regained his memory. He's been working as a joiner in France."

Victoria handed Rosy a photograph.

"Look they've enclosed a photograph: it's your Father, Rosy."

"Oh, Rosy, I'm so happy he's alive," said Hanna, holding back tears.

Rosy looked at the man in the photo and felt the tears. He was tall and handsome, with a kind face. Her mum admitted to her that she had always felt as if he was still alive. She was going to France to see him, talk to him and she was taking lots of photographs with her. Hopefully, they would jog his memory and he would come home.

"I hope with all my heart that when he sees you, he will remember us." Rosy said to her mother the next morning in King Frost's study as they said goodbye.

Although he was a King, he was also a father and seemed to know exactly how Rosy felt.

"Don't worry child, I have the feeling that all will be well."

Rosy smiled, then followed him, and one of the servants, to her new bedroom, which was next door to Princess Jaclyn.
Rosy was on a happy cloud: she couldn't wait to do what the King had suggested.

"Go and explore the castle," he said. "This will be your home for a while, and we don't want you getting lost, do we?" he smiled.

"No Sir!"

"Jaclyn is busy with schoolwork now, but she will meet you in about an hour in the library. It's on the ground floor, through the door marked library."

He laughed in a loud chuckling way, that made Rosy laugh too. He had such a nice smile, and he made her feel instantly comfortable and so welcome. She just knew she was going to love staying at the castle.

She hoped and prayed her father would remember her mother and return home with her. She had never known her father and was so excited at the thought of meeting him and telling him all about her life so far, and about all the things he had missed.

*

Rosy opened the huge library door and peered inside. The room was bigger than the gym hall in her old school. It had seven tall windows with coloured glass scenes of battles with soldiers wearing helmets and dragons breathing fire.
One window had what looked like a map of the Kingdom of Merry.

There was a large chunky log burning in the grate of the massive fireplace, which made the room feel really cosy. Above its mantle on the wall, was a shield and two crossed swords.

There were big, winged chairs, heavy cushioned couches, and small tables everywhere she looked. She had the feeling that she had been there before, but she knew she hadn't.

There were thousands of books, so many in fact, that two lifetimes wouldn't have been long enough to read them all.

Her eyes caught sight of a pile of what looked like blue school jotters stacked on one of the bottom shelves on the righthand side of the fireplace. She blew the dust off the one on the top of the pile and sneezed. It had smudges of ink all over the cover, but when she opened it to look at the first page, it was spotlessly clean, and the handwriting was so neat. Rosy's handwriting was anything but neat, as her teachers had told her many times.

She read...
Year 2,
Daily Journal of, William Achaius,
Stable boy,
1 Lakeside Cottages.

She wanted to see if Year 1 was in the pile, but she didn't like to look because she hadn't asked permission, and it wasn't polite to look through someone's books without asking. However, looking at the name on the book she was holding, it had been written by an Achaius, so she told herself it would be okay to read it as it was probably one of her relatives.

She turned the page and began…

December 5.30am,
It's a cold morning with a hard ground frost, which
may work in my favour. Today I must prove that I
am not afraid. Yesterday I ran, but not today.
Today, I will stand my ground. The King has given
me a birthday present of a fine sword. I must and
will prove myself worthy of his trust. William
Achaius

December 6pm,
Darkness always unleashes my fears, but I'll try to
hold on to the daylight in my mind. I will not give in
to fear: I am strong.

December 6.45pm,
Here he comes, his nostrils flaring: he's breathing
hard air at me. It's as if his nostrils are going to fire
balls of flames at me at any moment. He's such a
magnificent creature, but so dangerous. I can see
why people find him terrifying. Yet…, his eyes are
not showing any sign of anger. I know if he wanted
to, he could stomp all over me, and tear me into little
pieces. I wish there was some way of
communicating with him. How can I let him know, I
mean him no harm?

December 7pm,
He's backed himself into the corner. Surely, he must
have known there would be no way out for him from
there. I have a feeling that he is testing me. I'm

going to show him I'm not afraid of him. I'll sit down, wait, and see what he does.

December 7.30pm,
He's calmer now, but can I trust him? Wait...His eyes have changed colour. Strange, I've never noticed his eyes change colour before? He's coming toward me with his head down. I can't see his eyes now: his heavy double mane is covering them. Hold steady William, stand, and hold your ground.

December 7.40pm,
He's breathing on my face. I don't know if I can move, I feel as if I'm frozen to the spot?

December 7.45pm,
If he leans any harder against me, I'll fall over.

December 8.00pm,
He's not angry anymore, he's nuzzling my neck. He's allowing me to rub his nose, good boy, good boy.

December 8.30pm,
What a spectacular creature he is, and he's so affectionate. It's strange to think that all this time, I've been terrified of him. He must have thought I was being unfriendly. The King will be pleased that I've faced my fears.

December 6.00pm,

Tonight, he let me saddle him. The apple may have helped. He really loves the apples from the tree in our garden. I seem to have made a friend.
William Achaius.

She was about to turn the page to read more, when the library door opened, and one of the maids came in with a tray of biscuits and two cups of hot chocolate.

"I hope you love hot chocolate and butter biscuits as much as I do, Rosy?" shouted Princess Jaclyn, running in from behind the maid and throwing herself onto one of the couches in front of the fire.

Lifting a cup and a biscuit, she asked, "What are you reading?"

"Oh, I hope you don't mind," said Rosy, laying the book back on the pile and lifting a cup.

"This is a library Rosy; you're allowed to read any book. Search among them to wherever your interest takes you."

"Thank you!   I was reading about a stable boy, whom I'm sure must be one of my relatives, because his last name is the same as mine, and he lived in our cottage."

"That must have been an exciting find for you. Wait! Of course, your name's Achaius…Come with me!"

Then, with great excitement, she banged the cup onto the tray and ran toward the door. Rosy followed her, finding it hard to keep up.

They ran up a wide staircase and along a corridor that was so long Rosy wondered if it had an end. They climbed another staircase, then another. It was just one corridor after another until, at last, they climbed a small spiral staircase to a black wooden door. Jaclyn opened it with a key that she took from a nook in the wall.

The room was dim, and Rosy could barely see, but she knew it wasn't filled with treasure. In fact, there didn't seem to be any good reason as to why the door would be locked in the first place.
Jaclyn opened the huge shutters to let in the light, and Rosy gasped.

The ceiling and the walls were brightly painted with lots of different kinds of scenes. However, after closer inspection, she realised that it wasn't several scenes; it was one continuous scene.

Her eyes were drawn to a beautiful white horse and its rider. The horse looked exactly like Shem, but the rider was NOT the King.

Hanna gasped and squeezed Rosy's hand.

Rosy's eyes were scanning the huge painting her mind searching for a rational explanation of why someone would be painted riding the King's horse: no one rode the King's horse.

Princess Jaclyn noticed Rosy's bewildered look and smiled.

"It's William Achaius. The painting was done when he was in his twenties. He was Shem's special friend, and the only one, at that time, apart from the King, permitted to ride him."

Rosy was confused!

Rosy's not the only one confused! James shouted.

"Can the King ride the neugle horse or not?"

"Yes, James, he can, and if you can just practice a bit of patience, you'll find out more," answered Rosy.

"… Let me explain something to you Rosy," said Jaclyn.

"The family Achaius have been closely connected to the Frost family for many centuries. They have protected each other through wars, and many other dangerous situations. Part of our studies, my brother and I, is to learn the history of Merry Castle, the Frost family, and the history of the trustees. No one would ever be permitted to stay in the castle without my father knowing every detail of their historical past. You live in the number one cottage, which means that your family, are the closest to my father. Do you understand?"

The tears were running down Rosy's cheeks for she knew, in that moment, that it had to have been the King, who had found her father.

"Oh Rosy, I didn't mean to make you cry, I'm so sorry."

Rosy wiped her tears and smiled at the Princess. She explained that her mother had gone to France to see her father, whom they had believed dead for so many years. She now understood that it must have been the King who had found him. It wasn't her mother who was the trustee, it was her father.

Jaclyn smiled, knowingly, and gave Rosy a friendly hug.

"Let's go and annoy John," she said, holding out her hand, and they walked toward the door.

*

In the weeks that followed, Rosy became one of the Frost family: she knew that her time with them would never be forgotten. She had a comforting confidant in Jaclyn, a friend and protector in John, and King Frost was like the father she had never had, which made her constantly wonder what her own father would be like. Would he be coming home with her mother, she wondered?

*

One afternoon, after her ride, Rosy was brushing Kara when a stranger appeared at the stable door.

"Can I help you?" asked Rosy.

"Perhaps, I might be able to help you?" replied the stranger, smiling.

"I'm looking for my daughter, Rosemary," and he held open his arms.

It took Rosy a second for it to sink in, then she ran to him.
They held each other for a long time, both crying, with happiness. Rosy had never felt so loved.

"Oh, I'm so happy that her father's back home," said Hanna close to tears.

Rosy's mother was so happy to have her husband back home, and after a few weeks, the Achaius household was as it had always been meant to be.

Rosy's mother and father agreed with the King, to allow her to continue her studies with the tutor at the castle. Everyone agreed that she was much happier, even her handwriting had improved.

*

On the day, her studies resumed, her father started back at his old position working with the horses in the main stables at the castle. They walked home together most days, usually one of them remembering something new to talk about from the days gone by.

Jaclyn and Rosy rode together daily, Rosy listening carefully to the stories that Jaclyn would tell her about Mother Nature, Queen Spring, and her cousin Princess Snow: she also spoke of her distant cousin from Russia, Snegurochka.

The name was so unusual that it made Rosy question the pronunciation...

"Snegur...ka... what... can you say that again?"

Jaclyn laughed.

"Yes, it is a difficult name to say, Sneg-ur-och-ka, she's a Snow Maiden. Unlike Princess Snow, she doesn't bring the snow, she's made of snow, and before you ask, no, not like a snowman. She's very beautiful and her crown looks like a large sparkling snowflake. She always travels with my Grandfather Frost to Russia, giving gifts to the children. This year my Grandfather Frost is performing our Merry-Kiss, so you will meet them."

*

101

Rosy had been asked to help with this year's Merry-Kiss Ball.   Jaclyn had decided that everyone's costume was to be in the design of a flower and her dress had just arrived. It looked spectacular: as usual she had put a great deal of thought into the design.

She lifted the dress out of the box, "What do you think Rosy?"

Rosy thought that Princess Jaclyn was becoming so beautiful; what's more, she had a beautiful heart to match.
She stared speechless at the sparkling dress in total admiration of her friend's imagination: she loved snowdrops and the dress was exact.

When King Frost saw it, he said, that wearing that gown, she was going to make heads turn in the castle, which would make a change from heads rolling. Then he walked away laughing in his usual loud, chuckling, mischievous way

Rosy was really looking forward to the Merry-Kiss this year, she had a feeling that it was going to be amazing.   It was also going to be the first time she would be attending with both her parents.   Her twelfth birthday and her first Merry-Kiss dance with her father, she couldn't wait. It would also be a bit strange, because ever since her sixth birthday, she had danced the first dance, every year, with Prince John.

Rosy loved poppies, so her mother had made her a red satin dress with a black insert at the front: layers of red net underneath, which made it looked like a poppy in full bloom. She had green shoes and stockings, that made her long legs look even longer. The black hat fitted her head like a swimming cap: her mother had laughed and said, it topped the outfit off nicely.

Although Rosy loved her dress, she knew that the red didn't exactly match the shade of her long poker straight orange hair. Her choice of flower would have matched her hair better had she been a marigold, but she didn't care because the Ball was going to be amazing.

The men were to wear white suits, a bow tie, and a coloured sash of their choosing. That had been decided after a particularly heated discussion with Prince John, who argued, that it would not be appropriate to ask the men to come as flowers: especially since Grandfather Frost would be performing the Merry-Kiss.

Rosy had burst out laughing thinking about it; and then laughed hysterically as Jaclyn suggested that Grandfather Frost could go as a daffodil; and John a dandelion. John had stormed off with his hurt pride, embarrassed, and angry at them for making fun of him.

*

The night of the Merry-Kiss had been wonderful: Grandfather Frost could freeze things with a look, and a nod of his head.
The countdown; the Merry-Kiss; the fireworks; and then the birthdays; had all been, absolutely, amazing.

The King looked so proud dancing with his daughter, who looked stunning.

John was dancing with Snegurochka and he smiled as he waltzed by. Snegurochka looked so beautiful in her Lily style dress.

As Rosy watched them dance, she had the strangest feeling; a new feeling; one that made her catch her breath; one that made her feel quite sad; and one that made her wish that it was she who was dancing with John.

She squeezed her father's hand and waited for the music to start for the second waltz. She thought how dashing he looked in his white suit, with its wide yellow sash to match her mother's buttercup dress.
She felt very proud that she had her father back, and she waltzed, 1,2,3, 1,2,3, around the room: taking great care not to step on his feet. She was aware, that she wasn't feeling as happy as she ought to have been.

The dance finished and her father left her to go and dance with her mother. Rosy felt very confused about the way she was feeling, so she decided to go and find Princess Jaclyn. Jaclyn always found the perfect reason for everything, but she couldn't see her anywhere, so she went to get a glass of lemonade. Snegurochka and John were at the drinks table, and Rosy didn't feel like being sociable, so she turned around and walked back in the direction that she had come when John tapped her on the shoulder.

"Can I have this dance Rosy? I missed you earlier. I've gotten used to you stepping on my feet every year," he said, laughing.

Until that moment, she hadn't noticed that his sash was the same colour of crimson as her dress. He must've forgotten that she would be dancing the first dance with her father.

For some reason, unknown to her at that moment, Rosy was thinking, 'no, it's okay you're not forced to dance with me anymore,' when she spotted Jaclyn dancing. John had a firm hold of her hand and was leading her toward the centre of the dance floor.
Rosy had danced with John so many times that she didn't even have to think about what her feet were doing anymore. It felt like she was dancing with her feet off the ground.

The music went immediately from one dance to another, and they continued dancing. Rosy was really enjoying herself when she felt a tap on her shoulder.

"My turn," said Snegurochka, removing John's hand from Rosy's as she slipped in between them, nudging Rosy out of the way.

Rosy curtsied gracefully, and left the dance floor; smiling a smile, that she didn't feel.
She made her way to the drinks table and lifted a glass of lemonade.

"Hello Rosy, isn't this year's Ball just wonderful? Look at all those beautiful gowns. Have you ever seen so many different colours of flowers?"

"Your dress is the most spectacular out of them all Princess Jaclyn."

Rosy always addressed Jaclyn in the formal way when they were not alone.

"I'll second that," said a voice she didn't recognise.

"Rosy, this is Prince Ionan from Calegonia."

Rosy smiled and curtsied politely: realising that this Prince was the reason Jaclyn had such a happy starry-eyed look.

"Oh, Happy Birthday Rosy," she laughed. "I almost forgot; how could I have almost forgotten your birthday?" she laughed again.

Rosy wished Jaclyn a Happy Birthday in return, then excused herself, leaving the two staring into each other's eyes. She could hardly wait to meet Jaclyn the next day to find out all about the Prince.

She wandered out into the garden: where all the memories of the past years came flooding into her mind. She was now twelve; but standing there in front of the fountain; its water dancing with different colours in time to the music; she felt as if she was that six-year-old again. She could still feel the magic of the gardens, and admired the sparkling white dresses of the trees, hugging the castle walls.

"Beautiful, isn't it?" said John.

"I saw you come outside, and I came to wish you a Happy Birthday."

He bent down, kissed her cheek, and handed her a small silver box with a red bow: "this is for you," he said, smiling down at her.

"And a Happy Birthday to you too, Prince John," she said jokingly, taking the small box and curtsying.

"Thank you very much, but you know we don't buy each other gifts."

"It is John to you Rosy; no matter where we are; or who is listening. It's just a small gift; I didn't buy it I made it for you; open it later. I won't be seeing you for a while. I'm to go north with Grandfather Frost in the morning: think of me sometimes."

And with that, he was gone, leaving her holding back tears with a huge lump in her throat.
She didn't like goodbyes.

She undid the red ribbon, opened the silver box, and smiled. It was a beautiful Christmas tree ornament: a wood carving of two children dancing.

She would treasure it forever.

Rosy Rides the King's Horse

When Rosy arrived at the castle the next day, she was told that school lessons would resume in January, after the holidays. She danced around the great hallway, so happy that she could now spend more time with Jaclyn, Shem, and Kara. However, her joy was short lived because Jaclyn and King Frost had left for Calegonia, at the invitation of Prince Ionan. Jaclyn had left Rosy a letter explaining that there had been no time to come to see her, but she would have lots to tell her when she returned. The tears flowed without end as she walked down the road toward home. She didn't understand why she was feeling so sad, because she was very happy for Jaclyn, and for John. She told herself not to be so silly and dried her eyes.

At the bottom of the hill, instead of going home, she turned toward the watermill. Going to the stables to visit Shem and Kara always made her feel happy, and they looked forward to an apple. She had neglected them lately because of all the extra work helping Jaclyn with the Merry-Kiss.

She looked into Shem's eyes as she gave him his apple and knew that he understood her sadness. His eyes flashed with a beautiful shade of green, the colour of forgiveness and love.

"So… it's just you, me, and Kara," she told him, stroking his nose gently and giving him a kiss.

"Everyone's gone until after the New Year, which means that you won't have your daily ride with the King. I'm sorry about that, but you can come with us, when I take Kara for her exercise."

Shem neighed his approval, and Rosy left saying she'd see him the next afternoon.

The next morning, she felt much better, and helped her mother with the housework. She organised her clothes cupboard; boxed up some things to donate to the jumble sale; then helped prepare dinner.

Rosy was just about to head over to the stables when Kara appeared at the gate. She was used to Shem arriving alone, so she didn't give it much thought. She stood on the wooden stile, mounted, and clicked her tongue.

"Let's go have some fun, Kara," and off they rode in a gallop, toward farmer Anderson's lower field at the far side of the loch.

Rosy loved riding in the crisp winter frost, but she hated the dark nights. It was after seven by the time they returned. She dismounted, and stroked

Kara's neck lovingly as they walked toward the barn door.
Her father was in Kara's stall, with his back to her, opening a new bale of hay.

"You look busy?" she called out.

"Thought I'd give you a hand," he shouted back, cutting the string with his penknife.

"I'm just getting Kara settled for the night."

She was about to tell him that she was going to brush her first, when Kara whinnied from inside her stall... Rosy froze...

It must have been a full minute before she could move.

She lifted off her saddle and turned to find herself looking into Shem's beautiful green eyes.

She was in complete shock and couldn't think what to do.

Was there even anything that she could do?

She was staring at him, her mind racing.

Why would he do that?

Why would he do that to her?

Or more to the point...

How was it possible that she had ridden him and been able to dismount?

Her father was still busy in Kara's stall, so Rosy assumed he would think that she and Shem had been out walking.

"Change back now, quickly." She whispered into Shem's ear.

Shem changed into himself, and Rosy led him into his stall. She was silent while she brushed and fed him.

Shem constantly leaned into her, and she knew he wanted love and reassurance that she wasn't angry with him, but she was still in shock and couldn't find the right words. She kept thinking, how was it possible that she could have ridden him and then dismounted? He was her friend; how could he have played such a terrible trick on her?

She walked silently home, half listening to her father chatting about his day, wondering if she should tell him or not.

She decided the best thing to do, would be to leave it until the next day. Her mother always said that if she had a problem, 'sleep on it' everything always looked brighter in the morning.

Rosy left the house early the next morning before her parents were awake. She needed to go and find some answers, she was happy that she didn't have to explain where she was going, or why she was going. She needed to understand what had happened before she told either of them.

She walked quickly, with a purpose, up the winding road toward the castle.

*

The huge wooden door scraped across the tiled floor, echoing through the great hallway. One of the maids looked up from cleaning the legs of a table, and shouted:

"Morning Rosy."

Rosy shouted, "Hello," and waved, while continuing in the direction of the library. The fire had been lit, and the library felt cosy as she entered. Until that moment, she hadn't realised how cold it was outside. The stack of blue journals that she had looked at on her first visit to the castle library, were the first of many stacks along the bottom shelf. She lifted the one on top of the first pile, recognisable by the smudges of ink, and turned the pages slowly until she reached something familiar…

December 6.00pm,
He let me saddle him for the King. The apple may have helped. He really loves the apples from the tree

in our garden. I seem to have made a friend.
William Achaius

She turned the page and read the rest of the journal.
There was nothing out of the ordinary. Just his
normal daily routine and how he was becoming best
friends with the King's horse.
She picked the next book off the pile, but it was a
different name, and different cottage number. She
felt upset and confused as to why there were no
dates.
She skimmed through the first page from each
journal in the pile but none of them had William's
name. She craved the answers to so many questions,
but there was no one she could ask. One after
another, she searched through each pile, without
success.
She had just about given up when the library door
opened, and one of the young maids entered carrying
a tray with a large cup of hot chocolate and a plate of
cookies.

"You must be lonely without the Princess and the
Prince to talk to, so I've brought you a comfort drink
and some of your favourite biscuits."

Rosy smiled and thanked her.

If the truth be known she had forgotten about Jaclyn,
she was so busy trying to find William's journals.
She didn't know why, but she had a feeling that if
she could only find the rest of his journals, she

would get all her answers: after all he had ridden him too.

She gazed into the fire, whilst drinking her cocoa and watched the flames dancing away up the huge chimney. A sadness filled her heart, she couldn't help thinking if only Jaclyn and John were there, they'd know what to do.

She searched again for William's name among a few more stacks of journals, before giving up and heading for home.

By the time Rosy arrived home, it was almost teatime. Her mother looked a bit concerned when Rosy threw herself onto the kitchen chair. Laying her knitting needles down on the table, she got up and filled the kettle.

"Okay Rosemary Achaius, the kettles on for a nice cuppa, now tell me, how I can help you with whatever that load is that you're carrying around?"

"Has father gone back to work yet, because I really think you both need to hear this?" she replied.

Revelations in Time

Rosy gave her mother and father a detailed account of the previous day and they stared at each other in a moment of silence, then her father burst into laughter, while her mother giggled into the palm of her hand.
Rosy could feel her anger rising. She was in no mood for anyone making fun of her, or perhaps they were thinking that she was making up stories.

"I swear to you I'm telling you the truth," she shouted at them.

"My sweet girl," said her father, "of course you're telling us the truth, your mother and I would never think otherwise of you. I'm sorry for laughing. We were merely laughing from happiness because you have now come of age. I'll grant you, you're only twelve and that's a bit younger than the normal, but then you got to know him earlier."

"Eh… Mother…What do you think of our Rosy?"

Rosy looked first at one then at the other, now even more confused than before the conversation started.

"Can you please tell me what you're talking about?"

"Yes, please tell us what you're talking about?" James added, smiling.

"Okay," said her father, for starters... 'William' whose journal you've been reading, was my grandfather. Our Achaius ancestors have lived here for generations. In fact, I believe that at one time, they lived in the castle. I read something about it in one of the journals in the castle library when I was a child: but I don't remember the reason they lived in the castle. It could have been because, every now and then, the Frosts leave for a few hundred years and in their absence, the castle is looked after by a family of importance or even royalty."

"HaHaHa… Not that I think for a moment that our Achaius family were so important, or that we came from Royal stock."

He laughed again.

"No… they were more likely to be looking after the stock."

Rosy laughed.

"When I was a child, Prince John and I used to have imaginary sword fights in the great hall. He used to call me Prince Achaius."

"Wait! What? Prince John?" Rosy was growing more confused.

"Not young Prince John, his father, King Jack. We used to play together when we were young. He was Prince John then, but after he was crowned King, he became King Jack. I know it's very confusing Rosy, but everything will become clear soon I promise."

She lifted a cup of tea from the tray her mother had laid on the table, and as she sipped the hot sweet tea, she listened carefully to her father's story.

He had lived in number one cottage until he was eleven.
When he finished his primary education, he had been sent to live with his grandmother in the city, to finish his secondary schooling and perhaps learn a trade. Instead of returning to the cottage, when his schooling was finished: he found employment as an apprentice joiner with a friend of his grandmother. He had met Victoria, the joiner's daughter, and from there, Rosemary knew the rest of the story.

"So, when did you become of age: whatever that means?" asked Rosy, interrupting her father.

"Ah... yes... that, well... I was fifteen and on summer break from school. I loved working with the horses and rode almost every day with Prince John. We would race each other across the fields, which of course he always won. Then, on the day of my sixteenth birthday, Prince John, gave me a beautiful black stallion. I couldn't accept it of course, I lived in the city and it was far too much. I told him I could only look after it when I came home, but I would ride him as often as I could. I have to admit to you," he smiled in remembrance. "It did bring me home more often. Well...it did until I began courting your mother," he smiled again, but this time straight at her mother. It was such a loving look that Rosy was reminded of how much her parents loved each other. It gave her a warm feeling and she hoped that one day she could find such a love.

Her father continued...

"It was the last day before returning to the city and I was picking a couple of apples from the tree in the garden when Prince Achaius, my black stallion, arrived at the gate. Yes, Rosy... just like your Kara did with you. We rode like it was a race, with the wind behind us trying to catch up. It was a truly wonderful day, but when we arrived back at the stables and I saw Prince Achaius, still in his stall. I was in complete shock just as you were. Fortunately for me, I had Prince John waiting in the stables to explain it. Sadly, for you I didn't see you arrive back, or I would have known immediately what had happened."

Rosy smiled and took her father's hand.

"It seems that this Neugle can allow its chosen friends to ride it free of the Neugle's curse. The initiation, or as I call it the coming of age, must happen without the friend's knowledge."

Rosy was shocked to say the least.

"What would've happened had I recognised that it was him, and not Kara?"

"Ah…well, that I can't answer, because it's never happened: not that I know of anyway. However, on a positive note, you can now ride him any time you wish without fear. He'll enjoy taking the disguise of whatever or whomever you wish him to be. You're a very fortunate young lady indeed, and of course you must also know that one day you will become the next trustee of number one."

Rosy had always known that she would inherit the family cottage because her mother had told her, when she was a child.

"One day Rosy, this will all be yours. Make sure and give it plenty of loving care and in return, it will take care of you," she had said it many times.

Rosy had another cup of tea and nibbled on a biscuit, while she thought about how this revelation would change her life.

"WOW!" shouted James.   "I can't believe you can ride a Neugle Rosy!"

"Hold on a minute young man, I never said that Rosy was me, and I've never said that this story is true!"

"Please tell us more, Rosy. I'd really like to know what happens next?" Hanna asked, in a sweet little pleading voice.

It was Rosy's father's first Christmas back and her mother had made everything extra special which had been thoroughly enjoyed by all. Rosy had been allowed to stay up to see in the New Year with a small glass of sherry, which had made her feel very grown up, but very sleepy. The first footing around the neighbour's houses had not taken place. It had been decided that the first foot bottles, were to be donated for the New Year's dance in the village hall, and everyone would meet there. The dance had been so much fun. Rosy loved dances like, the Gay Gordon's, and the Dashing White Sergeants, although, it would have been so much more fun had Jaclyn and John been there.

Coronation Year

The holidays were over at last and Rosy arrived at the castle for her first school lesson of the new year. Jaclyn threw her arms around her and told her how much she had missed her; adding that so much had happened, and she was dying to tell her all.

"Stay overnight so we can have a girlie night and catch up?"

Rosy had her own major news, but to Jaclyn it would probably not be as exciting as her Prince, which for some reason made Rosy think of John.

"I haven't seen John today," she said, giving Jaclyn a questioning look...

Rosy was sitting close to the fire, her cheeks felt as if they were burning.
Jaclyn explained that John would be in training with Grandfather Frost for several years, but perhaps he would return occasionally for a holiday, or for the Merry-Kiss.
Rosy tried to hide her disappointment as she sat listening to Jaclyn talking about her handsome

Prince; how lovely his family were; and how his castle was much bigger than Merry Castle. It seems they had even discussed marriage, which Rosy had said was very fast.

"When you know you know, Rosy. I really love him so much." Jaclyn told her, with a glow in her cheeks and a faraway look in her eyes.

Rosy didn't know how to feel. It was as if she had lost her two best friends and hadn't seen it coming. She hadn't had the time to prepare herself for such a loss, and didn't know how to react, or what to do. The rest of the week was a mixture of highs and lows, until Rosy's mind had processed all the changes: and she had come to terms with the fact, that everything must change. Her mother had told her that change could be a good thing, but that's not how Rosy felt.

*

The months flew by as if they had wings and Prince Ionan arrived to spend Easter with them. Rosy had fully expected not to see much of Jaclyn during those days, but she had been wrong. On most of the days, they all went out together, riding or cycling to the ice cream parlour in the village square. She could see why Jaclyn loved him. He was very easy to talk to, so funny and not at all snobbish.

*

The day before he was to leave, they all went into the city to the new cinema. The Pathe News was showing the preliminary arrangements being made, for   the up-and-coming coronation   of   Queen Elizabeth.   Rosy got her first glimpse inside Westminster Abbey, London, where the coronation was to take place.

Prince Ionan's family had an invitation, and he had asked the King if Jaclyn could accompany him. King Frost had said they too had invitations, and he thought it better that Jaclyn accompany him and her brother. Jaclyn had been a little bit disappointed, but she understood and told the Prince that she would see him on the day.

When Prince Ionan left to return home, he took Rosy to one side and asked her to please be extra kind to his beautiful Jaclyn. He didn't want her to feel too sad, and miss him too much, when he was gone. It filled Rosy's heart and made her smile as she promised she would keep her happily occupied until they saw each other at the coronation.

*

The week before the coronation, the King bought three new-fangled boxes called television sets and set them up in the great hall. He explained that the British Broadcasting Company were filming the coronation, and whoever wanted to, could watch on the television screen, as it was happening. Everyone was so excited to watch it on the small television screen. It was much better than having your ear pressed onto the front of the wireless set.

Rosy had been looking forward to seeing John, but he hadn't arrived. He told Jaclyn that he thought it best to travel with his grandfather, and he would meet her and his father there.

Rosy joined her mother and father; some of the staff and their families, at the castle. Everyone sat with her eyes glued to a screen, trying to catch a glimpse of a familiar face. Her mother had said it would be easier finding a flea on a cat which had really made Rosy, and her father, laugh out loud.

The Coronation had gone smoothly apart from a little rain and the new Queen Elizabeth the second now sat on the British throne.

Rosy's father had said that the new Queen was beginning her reign in a changing world which Rosy didn't fully understand but the Queen was certainly beautiful and everyone watching her coronation was happy for her.

*

When Jaclyn arrived back, she was glowing, but Rosy thought that was probably more to do with the fact that she had seen Prince Ionan, rather than the coronation, and she was right. She confided to Rosy, that after a long conversation between King Harold and her father, they had agreed on a possible marriage taking place between Jaclyn and Prince Ionan.

It had been agreed that Jaclyn must first, finish her schooling. If she and the Prince still felt the same, then the marriage would take place on Jaclyn's twenty-first birthday.

"Wow!" Exclaimed Rosy.

"I know Rosy, I'm so excited. I love him more every time I see him, but my twenty-first birthday… it's a lifetime away. "

She threw herself onto her bed, like a fainting film star.

"Don't be so dramatic," said Rosy laughing.

"The time will go by very quickly, you'll see."

                              *

The following one and a half years went by like a lightening flash, with the Prince coming for summer and Christmas, and Jaclyn going to Calegonia, for New Year and Easter.

The Neugle Hunters

It was Rosy's fifteenth birthday and Jaclyn came to find her during the Merry-Kiss Ball. It would be exactly one year until her wedding and she wanted to ask Rosy to be one of her bridesmaids. Rosy was absolutely thrilled at the thought of being a bridesmaid at a Royal wedding. Jaclyn confided that she was thinking of her wedding to try and cheer herself up, because John had not arrived to join the countdown: and she was really missing him.

Rosy confided that she too was missing him because standing on his feet during the dance was something she looked forward to every year.

Jaclyn had laughed out loud, and everyone had turned around.

Rosy asked if she'd like to go for a ride the next day, but Jaclyn said that they were all leaving in the morning to go to Calegonia for Christmas and New Year and would be gone until mid-January.

There was a part of Rosy that felt sad, but another part that didn't. The absence of the King meant that she could have Shem all to herself while he was gone.

The next morning Rosy was busy cleaning out the stalls at the mill stables when she heard a loud commotion outside and ran to see what was happening. Her father was holding a young man's arm behind his back and told her to go and call the police. Rosy ran immediately but not before she got a good look at the man. She had never seen him before and wondered what had happened.

She called the police and returned to find her father on the ground unconscious and no sign of the man. She screamed out to her mother to call an ambulance.

*

As Rosy's mother climbed into the ambulance to be with her husband she called out instructions to Rosy to stay inside the house and wait for the police. She would call her as soon as she knew something.
Rosy went into the house immediately and locked the door.
Who was the stranger and what did he want?

She had wanted to go to check the stables but being alone she thought she'd better wait for the police.

When the police arrived, she explained the little she could, which wasn't very much. They would have to talk to her father for the whole story. The Sergeant said he'd go to the hospital and wait. Perhaps it would be possible to speak to her father when he was conscious.

Constable Dickson from the village was instructed to stay with Rosy, until he returned.

While Rosy made the constable some tea, he told her that he had heard reports over the past week, of two strangers hanging around the village.

"We had a report yesterday, just before the countdown that two men were asking some of the villagers if they knew of any available jobs at the castle stables. It's not normal to find strangers walking among us, especially ones that no one knows anything about. The King always knows something, but he left this morning."

"Yes, I know," said Rosy, "they won't be back until the middle of January."

"Well, don't you worry Miss, we'll be doing regular checks from now on, at least until we find out what's going on."

*

Fortunately, Rosy's father was fine, apart from a headache, and he was allowed home after a check-up.   He had a large bump on his head where someone had hit him from behind, but the doctor said it was nothing to worry about.   The X-ray hadn't shown any damage therefore he could take something for the pain if his headache got worse.

Sergeant Rogers had brought them home and after a warm drink, her father did a reconstruction of what had happened.
They looked around the stables for anything out of the ordinary but found nothing.
After a discussion on the safety of the horses, it was decided that Kara, Woolly and Shem, be taken to the stables at the castle.   The Sergeant said that no one knew what these men were after, and until they knew more, or the men were caught, it was better that a guard be posted.   He had requested police officers to be sent from the city to help.
Lakeside village didn't have a resident policeman because nothing ever happened.   However, this was a major incident and within hours the whole village was buzzing.   There would be no hiding place for these men: someone was bound to see them.

Rosy was settling Shem in his stall at the castle stables, when she had the most awful thought…

What if these men were Neugle hunters and that's why they had been at Neugle mill?
She went immediately to tell her father; he was seeing to Kara and Woolly in another part of the stables.

"You know my girl, that never crossed my mind, but now that you mention it, I suppose the possibility of it, can't be dismissed. I'll go and tell the Constable and you go and have a word with Shem so that he can be on the lookout, just in case."

Shem's eyes flashed red, brown, and grey when she told him. She couldn't think of anything, that he or she could do, that would help the situation. She knew that he would now be worried about Kara, but it was better that he knew to be careful.

Her father locked up and they slowly walked home. There was no moon, and it was dark. The ice was thick on the pavement, so they walked on the road. Rosy had the strangest feeling, that they were being watched, and she felt very uncomfortable. She was so worried about Shem and was wishing that she had stayed with him.

They had just finished supper when they had a call from the Sergeant. He had arrived at the stables to find Constable Dickson tied up, and Kara missing. Rosy was beside herself with worry and ran to get her coat and boots. She was out the door before her father had his boots on.

She ran like the wind up the castle road and threw her arms around Shem's neck when she found him still in his stall.

Oh, why hadn't she thought to leave them in the same stall? She was so angry at herself and felt so helpless.

Shem immediately took to the sky, in the form of a beautiful eagle. Rosy knew that he was the only one who could find Kara.

She wasn't worried about him; she was worried about what he would do to the men if they harmed Kara. She had awful visions about what the newspaper headlines could be.

'Men mauled to death by unknown beast. The army has been called in to search and kill.' She shuddered, wrapped herself in a blanket and tucked herself into the corner of his stall to wait for his return.

He hadn't been gone long when he came trotting into the stables with Kara, who seemed none the worse for her ordeal.

Rosy ran to the stable door and called to her father and Constable Dickson to come, then went back to Shem.

'Oh, if only the King or Prince John were here to talk to him,' she thought.

Shem's eyes were still flashing red and black, and she knew that he was angry.

"You haven't been long," she said to him, "you must have found her close by."

He snorted and stomped his foot twice.

"Was she as far away as the village?"

He snorted again and stomped once.

"The mill? Was that where she was?"

Two stomps.
She knew that they had taken Kara to the mill, but she didn't know why.

She told her father that he should really go home and rest. There was nothing that could be done until morning. She would stay there, with Shem and Kara until morning, and to tell her mother not to worry.

"There are two Constables here to protect me and they'll be right outside the stable door."

Her father hugged her and left for home.

Rosy wrapped herself back into her blanket and went back into the stall. She was hugging Shem's neck, and reassuring him that all would be fine, when she heard a man cough behind her. Fear took hold of her, and her heart began to race.

She turned quickly to look at the stable door.

"That tartan blanket really suits you Rosy," said John smiling.

Rosy felt such a relief at seeing him; she ran to him; threw her arms around him; and began sobbing uncontrollably.

All her fears came pouring out with her tears.

"Oh Rosy, I'm so sorry, I didn't mean to frighten you." John said, holding her close.

"I've just arrived, and Constable Dickson filled me in on what's been happening. I should have been here for the Merry-Kiss, but I got held up. I was hoping to have been here this morning before my father and Jaclyn left, but thanks to my cousin Princess Snow, it wasn't to be."

Rosy took a step back and wiped her eyes.

"I'm sorry John, I just got a fright. I've been so worried, and I was just thinking that if only you or your father were here to talk to Shem: and here you are."

" ...And here I am," he smiled; and gently moved her hair away from her face.

His smile held such warmth that she smiled back and felt immediately safe.

"Do you trust me Rosy?" he asked her, lifting her chin until their eyes met. She felt his eyes penetrating deep into her soul, and she nodded.

"Very well, I have an idea."

As Rosy listened to John telling Shem of his plan, she was amazed that she understood exactly what was being said. Was that because she was really listening, and not just asking him yes or no questions, or had he and Prince John given her the gift of understanding?

These were questions to ask John later.

John was locking the bottom and top doors of Shem's stall door, when Rosy came out of Woolly's stall.

She waited, and as they walked out of the main stable, John raised his voice and winked at Constable Dickson.

"Come and have a hot drink gentleman, everything will be well for a few minutes?"

They all went into the castle where one of the maids was waiting in the kitchen with tea and butter biscuits.

While they were all enjoying the hot tea, John asked the Constables to please follow the instructions that he was about to give them.

They were to go to Shem's stall where they would find not Shem but Kara: then they were to take her to Neugle mill: leave her in her stall in the stables, and then leave. He and Rosy would be right behind them so not to worry.

They reluctantly agreed because it went against their orders from the Sergeant. However, John assured them that he would take full responsibility, and not to worry.

John told Rosy that no matter what happened, when they reached the stables, she was not to touch him. She was confused, but knew he had a reason and a plan.

The Constables left and Rosy put her coat and boots back on. However, before John's plan could be put into action, they heard the roaring and screeching of an animal. It was coming from the stables. They ran across the courtyard, and caught up with the Constables, who were just opening the main stable door.

"Don't open Kara's stall door?" John called out to them.

When they got to the stall door John turned to Rosy.

"It's best if you stand back?"

He knelt, took a breath, and lightly blew under the stall door: then he slowly opened it.
The two men who were about to come running out, were standing shivering in their frozen boots which were stuck to the floor of the stall.

The air was smoke-filled, and there was a smell of burnt fabric and singed hair: but no sign of a fire. The straw on the stall floor, was wet, and there was a small stream of water trickling out of the stall door. The two men drenched, soaked to the skin. Their clothes singed with burn holes: one of the men had no eyebrows.

Kara began to whinny, and stomped her feet, in the stall.

The terrified men, visibly shaken, began babbling. One man was asking a constable, not to allow the dragon to get them. The other shouting about the huge dragon, with the red eyes, breathing fire onto them.

A Constable handcuffed the two men together, while the other went to call for a Police van.

While they waited, John whispered something to each of the men, and put a finger to his lips, when they left.

"They'll never return," said John.

They stood in silence as they watched the police van leave, then they walked back into the stables in time to see Kara changing into Shem.

"I don't know what you did my old friend, but you really did frighten the lights out of them. I don't think they'll be trying to find a Neugle again, they'll be too afraid they'll meet the dragon."

John and Rosy laughed.

John said Shem could just settle there with Kara for the rest of the night and return to Neugle mill in the morning.

"In the morning," laughed Rosy.   "It's almost 4.00am."

They said goodnight to Shem and Kara and quietly walked back to the warmth of the kitchen, where Rosy made another drink.

They chatted until daybreak, John telling her all about his grandfather and his training. He asked her if she'd like to go for a ride later in the day, as he wasn't leaving until the day after.
She said that would be perfect and he drove her home in his new motor car.

"Phew, that was really exciting, wasn't it Hanna? Can you just imagine Shem, turning himself into a fire breathing dragon?" Said James.

"It really was, and I'm so glad that Rosy's father and Kara were all right. Is that the end of the story, Rosy?"

"Do you want it to be the end?"

Both children shouted no at the same time, which made Rosy smile before continuing…

*

It was almost six in the evening when Shem arrived at Rosy's gate. She wondered if she should go and saddle Woolly and leave Shem for John. She decided to wait until John arrived and ask him. She was amazed when John arrived and said that he wasn't permitted to ride him, because of the Neugles curse. It seemed that the curse could only be lifted when a Prince became a King. However, he was so happy that Shem had given her the gift of his friendship.
He said, to be able to ride him must be amazing.

She really enjoyed their afternoon ride. The time spent with John racing across the fields reminded her of the times they had spent together as children.

John joined her and her parents for dinner, and then with a smile and a wave he was gone.

Celebrations & Weddings

Rosy was beginning to get excited at the thought of being one of Jaclyn's bridesmaids. All the details had been talked over and decided upon.

There was to be a traditional ceremony of, Vows and Blessings, in the small chapel in Merry Castle, on Thursday 13th of December at 3pm followed by the Merry-Kiss Ball. Everyone in the Kingdom of Merry, was to receive an invitation to the wedding and the Ball.

The main ceremony was to take place for the people of Calegonia, in Calegonia Castle a few days later.

Rosy had never left the Kingdom of Merry, and her excitement at traveling to another Country was beginning to build. Plus, being a bridesmaid at two Royal weddings, albeit the same people getting married, was so exciting she could hardly wait.
At first it was like a dream, but then when she was fitted for not one but two bridesmaid dresses, it all began to feel real.

The drawings of the dresses looked so beautiful on paper; she could hardly wait for them to be made. They were like evening gowns, the type that she had only ever seen in magazines or were worn by film stars. Rosy had never seen anything like them never mind being able to wear one. She felt happy that her boyish figure had filled out a little in the past year: at least now the dresses would have some shape.

What with the wedding; the reception; the birthday fireworks; then the Merry-Kiss Ball; she told herself she was going to have the most amazing sixteenth birthday.

*

The months leading up to the wedding went slower than she had imagined which gave her time to enjoy the last few months with her friend.

She had a bittersweet feeling about the wedding because Jaclyn would be moving to Calegonia and she would only see her when she came for holidays. Everything was changing faster than she was ready for. Happily, she still had Shem. She had outgrown Kara several years earlier but still took her for daily walks. Jaclyn had been so busy with planning her wedding that Rosy had taken over riding, Woolly. It wasn't like riding Shem, but he was always ready to take her on a journey, across the fields when she needed to escape for a few hours.

She still loved the rides she and Shem went on when the king was away. She could talk to him and she knew he understood how she felt. Sometimes, when she looked into his eyes, it was like looking at the sky on a dark night: seeing a thousand tiny stars changing colour: like the lights on a Christmas tree: she loved him so much and was happy he was her friend.

*

The wedding day was almost upon them: Jaclyn and Rosy were playing records in the lounge, Jaclyn had an amazing collection of records and some new ones had just arrived. Pat Boone had just brought out a song called Blue Moon which Rosy loved, but it made her feel quite sad, so she didn't like to listen to it when she was alone. She much preferred fast songs like Elvis's Hound Dog so she could dance and have fun without thinking too much about the lyrics. The records in the box of new arrivals seemed to all be ballads and some of them quite sad.

When she told Jaclyn what she thought of the new songs, Jaclyn just laughed and sung a verse of, Que Sera, Sera, then laughed again.

"Okay I get it," said Rosy smiling.

"I'm not so crazy about them either Rosy."

She knew before turning that it was Prince John. He was looking every bit as handsome as the last time she had seen him, almost a year ago.

Jaclyn ran to give her brother a hug, and Rosy smiled when he winked at her.

She had mumbled a "Hi," and then for some reason, felt a bit awkward.

She was about to ask him if he had any news to tell her when the hairdresser arrived. She turned around for a moment and when she turned back, he was gone.

The hairdresser showed them book after book with pictures of hairstyles.

Rosy looked at Jaclyn.

"I think I'll have something completely different!" she said. "I haven't had my hair cut since I was at primary school, so I think it's time for a change. Short hair is fashionable. What do you think Jaclyn? Shall I wear it up in a French roll, like Grace Kelly, suave and sophisticated, or shall I have a cropped pixie cut like Audrey Hepburn? Which film stars hair style would suit your vision and go with my bridesmaid dresses?"

Jaclyn looked at her not quite believing that she would really have her waist length hair, cut off.

"If you're really brave enough to go for a Hepburn cut, then I think it would really suit you. It would work well with your tiara, but Rosy it's up to you. It's a drastic step to have all of your hair cut off, but if it's really what you would like...?"

Rosy had looked at all the photos of short styles and loved the pixie cut on the film star, Audrey Hepburn. She wondered if she should perhaps run it by her mother first but decided against it, she would just talk her out of it.

"Think of the saving on shampoo and drying time. I'm going to do it."

The hairdresser examined her face, in detail, and then said that her oval face; beautiful large green eyes; small nose; and full mouth; would really suit the cut. Then added...

"Any-von vis your cheekbones and figure, Dahling, vould suit any-sing. He was looking her up and down and smiling. But you must be sure it's vat you really vant," he continued.

"It cannot be glued on, after it's been cot-off."

He pulled all her hair back from her face, examined it carefully, then dropped it.
It felt like a lead weight had been taken from her for a second, and in that moment, she knew that it was time.

She watched in the mirror as he cut her hair just above her shoulders and told her to get used to it. He said that if she really wanted the pixie cut, he would cut it when he came again, to do Jaclyn's hair for the wedding.

Rosy was happy with that decision: it would give her mother the chance to get used to her shorter hair before it was cut again.

Jaclyn's hair was layered, waved, and then pinned into a French roll, she looked stunning, and every bit the beautiful Princess that she was, and Rosy told her so.

"Prince Ionan is very lucky to be getting such a beautiful wife," she said. "And, talking of becoming a wife...Is there anything at all that you want to do before you become one? I mean, it's only the tenth, we've got three days left, we could maybe escape somewhere for a day, maybe even two?"

"You're crazy, Rosemary Achaius, and as much as I'd love to say yes, it's impossible, but why don't you come and stay in your old room until after the wedding, we can have some fun like we used to? My father's been having long discussions with your father and John about the Hungarian Revolution and I'm so bored listening to it all. It doesn't make for the romantic build-up to my happy ever after wedding day, that's for sure. If you come, we can learn some of the new dances, and we can celebrate our birthdays early with a bottle of bubbly?

Well, I can celebrate with bubbly, you can have orange juice," she said laughing.

Rosy loved the idea and went home to show her mother her new hairstyle, and to pack a bag. She knew her mother wouldn't mind as it would save her legs having to walk up the steep castle road every morning for the final fittings of her dresses.

The two other bridesmaids, one a little older and one younger than their cousin, Prince Ionan, weren't arriving until Tuesday. She wasn't sure if they would be like him or if she would have to be formal and polite, only time would tell. In the meantime, she could have two nights of fun with her friend all to herself, before she had to be careful of her Ps and Qs.

"What are Ps and Qs?" Hanna asked.

"It's just an expression that we use when we have to be more careful of what we say."

"I like that expression," added James. "I need to watch my Ps and Qs when I talk to grandfather."

*

…Rosy and Jaclyn had two wonderful fun filled days. In the evenings they played all the new records and practiced the latest rock n roll dances. Then it happened.

*

Jaclyn's special day arrived, and she could not have looked more beautiful.

The snowflake lacework of her wedding dress was so delicate it looked like a layer of frost shimmering over the pure white satin. She had designed all the bridesmaid's dresses herself and although they were all the same colour of apple white, they all had an overlayer with a shimmer of fir green. Each dress was a different design and Rosy had been fortunate enough to be able to choose which two designs she preferred, which had then been made to fit. She loved the dresses: she loved how she looked in them: and she loved how she felt wearing them.

The dress for the Merry Castle wedding had a narrow band emphasising her waistline with an array of emerald-coloured stones, that matched the rim of the lace bolero covering her shoulders. The hairdresser had cut her hair into the cropped Audrey Hepburn style, and Jaclyn had chosen some light makeup to suit her fair skin, along with a pale tangerine shade of lipstick. Rosy had never worn makeup, so when she stepped in front of the mirror, she stared at her reflection for a long time, in total wonder at the different person looking back at her.

The petit emerald tiara was a perfect match for the dress and sat circling the crown of her head, undisturbed by her new haircut.

Her mother's only remark on that subject, had been that at sixteen years of age, she was old enough to choose what she wanted to do with her own hair and that she thought that it would be much easier for her to manage.

Her father told her there was only six weeks between a good haircut and a bad one. He then said she'd probably have to buy a new riding hat as her other one would now be too big. Then he had laughed.

She couldn't have been mistaken at the many double head turns as she walked into the chapel behind Jaclyn.

She was floating on a cloud, but at the same time completely aware of so many eyes upon her from the chapel door to the altar, which she didn't like at all.

'Focus', she told herself, 'focus on your feet, and don't trip whilst carrying the train of Jaclyn's dress.'

She was relieved to lay down the heavy crystal layered train, and as rehearsed, took a few steps to the left then forward, just in time to be handed Jaclyn's bouquet.

Rosy smiled at her friend, gave her a tiny nod, and then she and the best man, Prince Baylor, took three steps back as Jaclyn and Ionan moved forward and kneeled onto the soft padded stool, to begin their traditional vows.

Rosy had to catch herself several times when she felt a tear coming during the ceremony. Jaclyn had given her a stern warning not to cry, or she would have brown mascara running down her cheeks. The very thought of which was enough to give someone nightmares.

The ceremony didn't take long but it was so beautiful.

The formal ceremony in Calegonia Castle would take several hours and although she was looking forward to the traveling and sightseeing in Calegonia, the actual pomp and ceremony of the wedding, was not something that she could feel excited about. However, she would do anything to make her beautiful friend happy.

*

In the evening just before the Merry-Kiss Ball, whilst Rosy was standing near the fountain awaiting the balcony appearance: she couldn't help thinking back. She was now a whole ten years older but really didn't feel any different. It was only her outer appearance that had changed, and she had more memories, but apart from that she still felt like the same Rosy inside. She still looked in awe and wonder at the world around her and thought how lucky she was to have been brought up in such an amazing place.

She felt a nudge and turned to see a waiter holding out a tray with several glasses of lemonade. He had the same beautifully mesmerising eyes as Shem. Shem had taken human form; she would have known those eyes anywhere.

She laughed and lifted a glass of lemonade.

"Cheers to the happy couple, and cheers to you, my lovely friend!" she laughed again and took a sip.

"Is that toast meant for me?" asked a voice behind her.

She lifted another glass from the tray and handed it to John.

"But of course, kind Sir," she laughed, and the two glasses clinked.

"In that case, I lift my glass to the most beautiful woman I know, both in looks and in heart."

Rosy turned around expecting to see Jaclyn behind her but there was only Shem in the distance.

"I'm talking to you Rosy?" he said and laughed.

"Do you really not know how beautiful you are? And, I have to say, your new hairstyle is amazing, I hardly recognised you."

She could feel her cheeks burning and she looked away, so she had time to think of a witty remark, but the fireworks began crackling in the sky above their heads for the birthday honours. They normally would have been the night before as the date changed but this year everything was different.

She turned around to wish him a happy birthday and the birthday kiss that she would normally have received on the cheek made contact with her lips. They stared at each other in silent shock for what seemed like forever, then John mumbled something under his breath and walked briskly away in the direction of the hall.

Rosy heard the music and knew that it was time for the father daughter dance, which this year was going to be the first dance of the new Mr and Mrs. Her cheeks were on fire and her legs were shaking as she entered the hall.

Jaclyn and Ionan were dancing, and people were joining in their dance. Rosie's father was dancing with her mother, and she smiled at them.

At that moment she felt a hand taking hers, gently pulling her toward the dance floor. She expected it to be John but instead it was Ionan's best man, Prince Baylor.

"I believe this one is the best man's dance, Miss Rosemary?" and he half danced his way onto the middle of the floor and bowed low, as if their roles were reversed. She laughed, curtsied, and they waltzed around the hall, dance after dance. She was happy to have the time to enable her to calm her thoughts, but her mind was still racing.

The kiss on her lips had been a simple accident, but she was sure that poor John must be feeling as embarrassed about it as her. He was one of her best friends, and she didn't want him to feel embarrassed when he was in her company. When the dance finished, she would go and find him and tell him that she understood that it was just a silly mistake, and not to worry about it. However, when the dance finished, Prince Baylor led her from the dance floor and handed her a glass of lemonade. He said they needed something sweet, for extra energy, so they could dance the rock n roll. Rosy thought he was joking and laughed, but then the music of Bill Haley began, and Prince Baylor pulled her back onto the dance floor. The lessons from Jaclyn really paid off, and Rosy danced the rock n roll like a professional.

Everyone clapped as they left the dancefloor when the dance finished and an embarrassed Rosy excused herself to go and find John.

She asked a few of the guests that she knew if they had seen him, but no one had seen him since the start of the Ball. Then she spotted her father and the King in the garden talking, and thought she'd just ask the King. She was walking toward them when her mother called out to her.

"Leave the men to talk, Rosy, and come and sit with me for a minute or two. I haven't had the chance to wish you a Happy Birthday, yet. Have you had a lovely day? You look absolutely beautiful and if I haven't told you before, I'm very proud of the young woman that you've become."

Rosy wasn't used to her mother expressing her feelings so openly and wasn't sure how to respond: She smiled and hugged her.

"Thank you, mum," she whispered, into her ear.

"Can I get a hug too," her father said, smiling?

Rosy stood and gave her father a hug.

"Can't have you feeling left out, can we?" she said, laughing.

"Oh, Before I forget, I have something for you," and he handed her a little red velvet box.

"What's this?" She sat back down to open the box.

"I was to give it to you earlier, but you were dancing. It's not from us, it's from Prince John. He said he would have given you it himself, but you were having so much fun dancing he didn't want to pull you away."

"Oh, Rosy, it's beautiful!" Exclaimed her mum. "I have a charm very similar to that; your father gave it to me after we had our first dance at our wedding."

Rosy was speechless.

"Have you seen Prince John; I'd like to thank him?"

"He's gone, Rosy. He left for Calegonia, about half an hour ago. He's part of the security team, on the train carrying the wedding gifts, luggage, and all the personal jewels and belongings of the Princess."

Until that moment Rosy hadn't given a great deal of thought to the technical details of Jaclyn moving away, and with John gone, what if the King moved too, what then! Her mind was racing again.
As she looked at the small silver charm of the couple dancing, she struggled to hold back tears.

Why hadn't he waited to say goodbye?

What was it with him, why couldn't he ever say a proper goodbye?

Then her mind turned to Shem, where was he…she hadn't seen him? Had he gone with John and the others to protect the Royal Treasures on the train?

Was that why he had taken human form?

"Penny for your thoughts?" said her father.

"I was just wondering where Shem was. What were you were talking to the King about, you both looked so serious?"

"We were just discussing him leaving with the Princess, Prince Ionan and the Calegonian guests, on the Royal train in the morning; and you, we spoke about you. You'll be traveling with them but returning with the King. We are to remain and take care of things here. You'll be formally announced as Princess Jaclyn's chief bridesmaid and representative of the Achaius Clan of Scotland.

"The conversation looked a bit more serious than that, Dad?"

"I can't tell you more than that Rosy. I'm your father, but you must remember that I am also a trustee, and there are some things I simply cannot speak of, not even to you!"

That uneasy feeling was gnawing away at her and it was getting stronger. She knew, she just knew that something was wrong, but for the life of her she couldn't think what it could be?

"Are you able to tell me if Shem is in his stable or is that top secret too?" she smiled and gave him a nudge.

"I believe he is with Prince John."

Rosy was now worried, but what could she do?

"Maybe she could leave and try to catch up with Shem and John on the train?" James answered, as if Rosy had asked him a question.

"I think she should do that too," Hanna agreed, looking a bit worried.

"And say what?" laughed Rosy.

"Well, I think she would have been better traveling with Prince John and Shem." replied James.

"Like the three musketeers!" laughed Hanna.

"Maybe time to stop now?" Rosy suggested.

"No!" They both shouted, "Continue… please."

Things Don't Just Disappear

Rosy woke very early the next morning so that she could go to the stables, she wanted to see Kara before she left. Kara had not eaten her food the day before and Rosy was a bit worried about her.

When she arrived at the stables, her father was already there. He told her not to worry, he had called Mr Simms, the local vet, to come and give Kara a check-up.

"Now, you'd better go and get changed, you don't want to be the reason that train doesn't leave on time. I'll call you this evening when we know something more. Go and have a lovely time and take lots of photographs; I've heard Calegonia is beautiful."

*

Rosy had never been on a train before, so her nose was almost glued to the window from the time they left Drallon station: she didn't want to miss anything.

It was amazing how much the scenery changed the closer they got to the Calegonian border. The Calegonian Mountain tops disappeared and all you could see was the mist.

The train was really struggling up the steep incline and Rosy felt uneasy as it entered the tunnel before Darnell station at the Calegonian border. She sighed with relief when the carriage filled with light and the train pulled into the station and came to a stop.

As she looked out of the carriage window, she was surprised to see each side of the rail track lined with soldiers which by the look on Prince Ionan's face he found strange.

*

When everyone had disembarked, and papers were being checked Rosy took the chance to walk around the pretty, colourfully painted station and take some photos with her little Brownie camera. The view from Darnell up into the surrounding mountains and down into the valley was spectacular and with each click of the camera, she tried to imagine how it must look in the spring, or in the summer, when it wasn't covered in a blanket of snow.

As she looked through the lens across the open plateau toward Darnell station and clicked the button of her camera, she felt a sudden chill. A cold wind was whirling around her feet and she began to feel, really, cold.

She took a few more photos as she walked quickly back to the train and after a cup of hot chocolate, she began to feel much warmer.

*

As she watched everyone get back onto the train, she suddenly realised that she hadn't seen Prince Baylor.

"Have you seen Prince Baylor, Sir?" she asked the King, as he sat down opposite her.

"I didn't see him get on the train."

The king looked over at Prince Ionan, who looked deep in thought, and asked him where Prince Baylor was.

"Oh, he left last night after the Ball, Sir. He had to be back for an early meeting this morning."

Rosy asked if he had gone with Prince John, and he said he hadn't, that he had left a bit later.

She wondered why he hadn't gone on the train with Prince John, but she quickly forgot, when the train began to pull away from the station, and her nose went back to its place on the windowpane.

*

When they arrived at Vourgo station, like the border crossing, there were soldiers everywhere. They were ushered, very quickly, off the train and into waiting cars.

Rosy had only just enough time to put her coat on and lift her bag before one of the escorts arrived.

There was a strange atmosphere that felt not at all welcoming, and Rosy began to feel a bit uneasy. The atmosphere should have been happier. She would have expected the people to be excited and looking forward to the Royal Wedding.

The King, sensing her anxiety, took her hand and smiled as if trying to reassure her, but even he was not his jovial self.

*

As they approached the castle and she caught her first glimpse, it was exactly as Jaclyn had described and more. It was at least three times bigger than Merry Castle, but it didn't feel anything like Merry Castle.

King Harold was waiting for them at the entrance and after a brief welcome asked King Frost and Prince Ionan to step into his study.

Rosy decided that she liked King Harold, he was a bit older than King Frost and had a large grey moustache that curled at the corners of his mouth. His eyes were stern looking but his laugh lines showed proof that he wasn't always as grumpy as he looked today.

As she watched them talking, Rosy began to feel that same uneasy feeling in her stomach that she'd had earlier.

Princess Jaclyn had just begun to ascend the wide staircase followed by a maid, when the Prince came hurriedly out of the study and called to her to come.

He turned and looked at Rosy: "You too Rosy."

King Frost looked very concerned as he looked at Jaclyn and began...

"There's no easy way to say this so here it is straight: the other train carrying your belongings, the gifts, and crown jewels hasn't arrived. No one has seen it since it crossed the border last night. King Harold has had his army out searching, but there's no sign of it anywhere."

"How on earth can a train just disappear?" Jaclyn shouted, then burst into tears.
Prince Ionan put his arms around her and tried to comfort her.

"It's all right Jaclyn we'll find all your things don't worry."

Hanna and James had been so engrossed in the story they hadn't heard the door open until suddenly a voice shouted out behind them...

"I'm not worried about my things, I'm worried about my brother, he was on that train."

Hanna got such a fright she jumped up and screamed.

"Oh mummy, you scared me."

"Do you know this story, mummy?" Asked James.

"Not all of it James, and I'm really sorry to disturb you all, but it's time to go for your fitting."

"Oh, please let us stay to hear what happens next?" James pleaded.

"I must know if Prince John and Shem are all right."

"Tomorrow, James," said Rosy.

"I'll be here at the same time tomorrow, waiting with lemonade and biscuits, to tell you some more of the story. I did tell you it was going to be a long story."

"Promise?" said James, giving her a hug.

"I promise!"

Rosy smiled to herself as she watched James hold the door open for Hanna.

Printed in Poland
by Amazon Fulfillment
Poland Sp. z o.o., Wrocław

75551113R00092